A DEEP CREAKING SOUND DREW HIS ATTENTION UP TO THE MANSION...

"The front door slowly yawned open, like an ancient mouth, sucking the air of the living into its dusty, decaying lungs. A faint blue light flickered from somewhere deep within the cavernous husk, but Jonas couldn't see anyone there. The door had opened by itself. "

ALSO AVAILABLE:

BOOK 2

The adventure continues as Jonas Shurmann and his partners, CatBob and Neil Higgins, race to break a hundred year old curse before it ruins their friend's entire life in *The Dusenbury Curse*.

BOOK 3

Jonas, CatBob, and Neil Higgins face their biggest adventure yet when Jonas finds a mysterious ring that turns his life upside-down and inside-out in *The Deadly Scarab*.

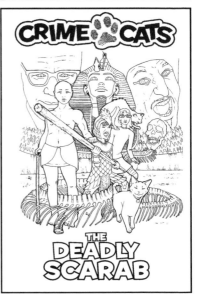

CRIME CATS

MISSING

Neil Higgins   CatBob

MISSING

WRITTEN & ILLUSTRATED BY
WOLFGANG PARKER

EDITED BY
MICHELE DOUGHTY

I would like to express my gratitude to the following friends.
Without their contributions, this book would not have been possible.

Kitty Maer, Ben Sostrom, Michele Doughty, Elizabeth Renkor PhD, Molly
Longstreth PhD, Doug Clay, Joseph Tramontana, Louise Santos,
Ross Hughes, Alycia Yates, Lee Nordling, Ronald Hanna,
Vinnie "Mad Chain" Maneri, Elizabeth Niswander,
Jonas Tonti, and the cats of Clintonville
and their wonderful families.

CRIME CATS: MISSING
Revised Text

RL 4. 008—012

Cover & interior illustrations by Wolfgang Parker
Cover colors by Ross Hughes
Crime Cats logo deigned by Alycia Yates

For permission requests, contact the author at
wolfgangparker@yahoo.com

Sixth Printing, 2015

ISBN 978-0615984698

15 14 13 12 11 10 / 10 9 8 7

PRINTED IN THE UNITED STATES OF AMERICA

To my nieces and nephews:

This book is a door into my world. Remember that it will always be open to you anytime you want to visit.

Merry Christmas and Happy Halloween,

~ W.P.

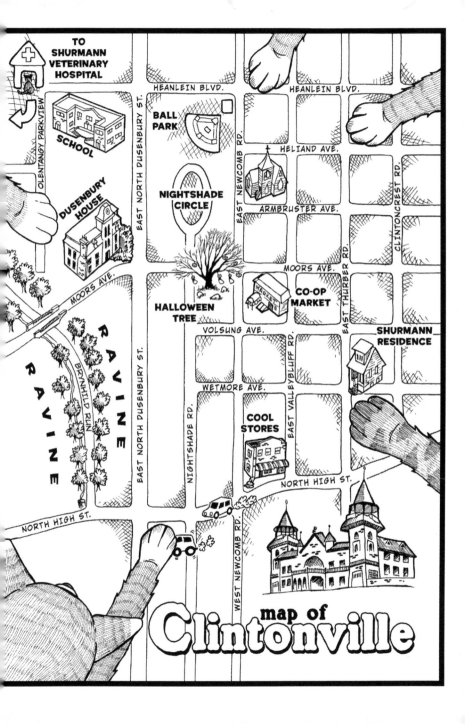

1

CHICKEN FEED

Jonas Shurmann woke up tired and grumpy—prob- *foreshadowing*
ably because he hadn't heard cats speak yet. He
hadn't saved Clintonville from the mysterious creature that terrorized the neighborhood. Nor had he yet
dared to enter the Dusenbury House or befriend the
ghost that haunted it. And no one called him a hero—
not yet. Jonas woke up an ordinary kid on that chilly
autumn morning: tired and grumpy, and *not* heroic.

He yawned a long, deep yawn, rolled out of bed,
and was shuffling toward the bathroom when he felt
something soft touch his face.

Jonas looked up to see his father holding before
him what looked like a cloth sack covered in white
feathers.

"Surprise!" Mr. Shurmann beamed. "It's for
your Halloween party at school today. What do you

think? Pretty cool, huh?" He held the costume up to Jonas's face. "The feathers feel real. Go on, feel 'em!"

Jonas reached out and gently rubbed one of the feathers between his thumb and forefinger. It felt real enough, but he wasn't excited about dressing in a sack covered in feathers. All he could muster was, "Wow. Yep."

Mr. Shurmann peered down at Jonas through his hexagonal eyeglass frames. The smile fell from his rosy cheeks.

"Ah, jeez, Jonas, I'm sorry," he said. "I went to the antique mall looking for something unique to surprise you with. The old woman who sold it to me said it was one-of-a-kind. She made a big deal about—" he frowned. "I guess I wasn't thinking."

Mr. Shurmann was dressed in bib-and-brace overalls. He wore a different, but identical, set almost every day. He called them his "business suits," because he wore them to work. Jonas liked that his dad worked from home, but he didn't like that his job caused him to worry so much.

Presently, Jonas noticed his dad's brows had knitted, turning his forehead into a mess of wrinkles. That always meant something was wrong. Usually, when Jonas would ask his dad what was worrying him he would reply, "work" or, "just adult stuff."

But despite the never-ending stress of work, Mr. Shurmann always made time for Jonas and Jonas knew not everyone's dad did. Jonas's friend Adam moved away when his parents got divorced. Jonas didn't know all the details, but he knew Adam wasn't very happy when he found out he would only see his dad on weekends. After that, Jonas always remembered to appreciate that his dad was there for him, even though he seemed to live on another planet sometimes—this being one of those times.

"It's okay, Dad," Jonas said. He took the costume and held it up to make a show of his appraisal. That's when he noticed the sack of feathers had a hood—with a beak attached to it!

Jonas bit his lip. It was one-of-a-kind, all right. He was sure of that. In fact, there was no need to ever make another one. Jonas couldn't imagine one kid wanting to be a chicken for Halloween, much less two. Still, he hated seeing his father disappointed.

Dressing up as a chicken for Halloween might have been popular when Dad was young, thought Jonas, *but things have definitely changed since then.*

"Are you sure?" Mr. Shurmann asked. "I know you said you wanted..."

"I'm sure," Jonas said, forcing a smile. "It's great, Dad."

"Well, I think it's adorable." Jonas's mom

appeared behind Mr. Shurmann. "Your lunch is packed and waiting for you on the counter, sweetie."

Most people recognized Mrs. Shurmann from the veterinary hospital where she always wore a white doctor's smock. But at home she wore T-shirts that exposed the colorful tattoos that covered her arms from shoulder to wrist. Dogs, cats, songbirds, fish, rabbits, and even a couple of Guinea pigs; each tattoo was a memorial to a pet she'd loved.

Jonas loved to lie in bed with his mom and look at her tattoos. Sometimes they would play a game where Jonas would point to a tattoo, and his mom would tell him a story about the pet the tattoo commemorated.

Jonas's mom was pretty cool most of the time, but the only thing Jonas thought was cool *this* early in the morning was more sleep.

"Okay," Jonas mumbled as he shuffled toward the bathroom.

"And don't forget you have work after school," she called after him.

"Uh-huh," Jonas grunted.

"*Right* after school, Mister. I need you to hustle your bustle, because we're super-busy, okay?"

"All right! Jeez!" Jonas dragged the sack of feathers into the bathroom and shut the door.

"I love you!" Mrs. Shurmann called. She turned to her husband. "He knows I love him, right?"

Jonas's dad looked glum. His brows had knitted again.

"Stop worrying," she said. "It's adorable. He'll be fine."

After recess, Miss Keys announced to her class that it was time to change into their costumes. Jonas went to the restroom where he spent ten minutes hopping and bumping around in a stall.

He'd worn the chicken costume under his clothes and the extra bulk made undressing awkward. Once he'd managed to wrestle free of his shirt and jeans, he took the chicken "feet" out of a crumpled paper bag and replaced them with his clothes. He slipped the feet over his sneakers and stood before the mirror to appraise his new getup.

Jonas looked like a chicken that had been deflated. The hood slouched over his eyes, the yellow beak sat askew, and the points of the comb (that red thing on the top of a chicken's head) flopped over to one side. It was a far cry from what he'd wanted to be for Halloween.

Miss Keys had instructed the class to dress up as whatever they most wanted to be when they grew up. Jonas told his father that he most wanted to be a hero. It didn't particularly matter what kind of hero he would be. He just knew that every story he'd ever read, every movie or TV show he'd seen, and every report he'd watched on the news, showed that everyone liked and admired a person who performed heroic deeds. And that's why Jonas wanted to be a hero, because he wanted to be liked.

Not that he was particularly *disliked* at school, but he tended to stand out for all the wrong reasons and this chicken costume was bound to be yet another. He would much rather have been a soldier, a fireman, a superhero, a knight, or a cowboy. Really, anything other than a chicken. To Jonas, dressing up as a chicken was the exact opposite of dressing as a hero.

Maybe not literally, Jonas thought, *because real chickens could be brave if they had to be. But people get called chicken for being scared, and no one would believe me if I told them I was a brave chicken, because no one's ever heard of one.*

Jonas heaved a sigh and shuffled out of the restroom with his crumpled bag of clothes.

He'd hoped his return to the classroom would go unnoticed, but as he made his way back to his desk, Jonas heard giggling and calls of "Bock-bock chicken!" He turned to find Danny Martin and his friends decked out in camouflage fatigues and green face paint. They were laughing and comically flapping their arms. Jonas pretended not to notice them. He stashed the bag and joined his classmates as the party got underway.

The kids bobbed for apples, took turns adding lines to a ghost story, watched a movie about the history of the holiday, then everyone received a small bag of mixed candy. That is, all except for the bag Jonas was given.

His bag had the words CHICKEN FEED scrawled on it and was filled entirely with candy corn. Jonas grimaced. When he showed it to Miss Keys, she held it up and asked the class who was responsible. The kids sat hunched over their desks, giggling and sharing secretive glances. Jonas tried to laugh along and insisted it was just a harmless prank.

He took the bag, popped one of the triangular treats in his mouth, and smiled weakly. "It's just a Halloween trick, see?"

Miss Keys frowned and returned to her desk. As soon as her back was turned, Jonas spit the chewed up candy into his hand.

"Blech!" he gagged. "A *disgusting* Halloween trick."

He crumpled the bag in his fist and stuffed it in his backpack. Jonas loved Halloween candy like every other kid, but something about the waxy texture and weird flavor of candy corn turned his stomach.   BULLYING

As soon as the bell rang Jonas rushed back to the restroom. His face was flushed and tears had begun to roll down his cheeks. He wanted to tear those feathers off and throw them in the trash, but when he caught sight of himself wrestling with the costume in the mirror he stopped. He thought about his father, how proud and excited he'd been when he presented it to Jonas that morning. Jonas's shoulders fell. He felt ashamed of himself.

He released the feathers, wiped his cheeks dry then hauled himself into a stall where he put his clothes back over the costume. He stepped out and heaved a sigh of relief when he saw the feathers were no longer visible, but unfortunately for Jonas, the party wouldn't be the last time they made trouble for him.

2
MISSING

Jonas hurried down Heanlein Boulevard to Shur-mann Veterinary Hospital where his mom worked. He'd started helping her during the summer for an increased allowance and had continued coming in a few days after school every week. He helped with baths, feedings, cleaning and filling water dishes, comforting the patients during exams and treatments, wiping down examination rooms, and prepping pets to go home, which was Jonas's first job when he arrived.

A fat, gray, one-eyed cat sat quietly in its cage studying Jonas as he prepared its carrier. When he noticed his furry audience, he knelt down and peered through the cage door. The feline met his gaze with a single amber eye. A lightning bolt-shaped scar was scored into the cat's face where its other eye should have been.

What a weird cat, Jonas thought.

Jonas didn't like cats. They usually drove him crazy pacing back and forth in their cages, constantly meowing. But the one-eyed cat seemed content to just watch him work. This was fine, at least at first. But after about five minutes of its creepy staring, Jonas decided he would rather the cat pace and meow like a normal cat—that would be less annoying.

This was just another in a long list of gripes Jonas had with cats. Since working at the vet's office, he'd decided cats were ungrateful monsters that had it far too easy in life.

As Jonas saw it, people were always fussing over cats like servants. Cleaning their fur off of clothes and furniture, scooping out litter boxes, and cleaning the carpet when cats threw up hairballs—which was like, all the time. Humans feed them, provide shelter, brush them, pet them, give them special treats, and for all of this, what do cats do in return? They pay no attention to anyone, they sleep all the time, and if you pet them too much, they scratch or bite you. Jonas just couldn't understand why anyone would want something as ungrateful as a cat for a pet.

Jonas opened the cage and scooped the gray cat up.

This cat may have one eye, thought Jonas, *but he*

never had to go to school in a ridiculous-looking chicken costume. He didn't get laughed at and get stuck with gross "chicken feed" candy corn. This cat probably has treats waiting for him at home.

"Cats have it easy!" Jonas sneered as he shoved the cat into the carrier.

"Hey, watch it!" a voice shouted.

The voice startled Jonas. He thought he was alone. He *was* alone, wasn't he?

"Who said that?" he called out.

Before an answer could come, he was startled again by shouting voices coming from beyond the lobby door. Jonas peered out the rectangular window and saw a sunburned man with wild, black hair at the receptionist's counter. He was waving his arms and yelling. Jonas cracked the door to listen.

"This is serious!" the man exclaimed, waving crumpled papers in his fists. "Puck's been outside for years and he's never wandered away from home—ever! He's a good cat."

The receptionist held a phone receiver to her chest and nodded. She tried to speak, but as soon as she'd opened her mouth, the man began shouting all over again.

"I don't think you understand!" he bellowed. "Something's in the neighborhood that shouldn't be here, and it might've gotten Puck!"

Jonas's mom appeared and took the man aside. Jonas wasn't close enough to hear what was said, but after a brief conversation the man seemed calmer and was nodding in agreement with whatever she was saying. He handed her one of his crumpled papers and left. She immediately pinned it to the bulletin board by the front door.

✳ It was a "missing cat" flier, but it wasn't the only one. In fact, Jonas couldn't find a spot on the board that wasn't covered by "missing cat" fliers.

Mrs. Shurmann then greeted a man with a bright smile and called back to Jonas to bring the gray cat out.

Jonas lugged the carrier over to the receptionist's counter then took a closer look at the bulletin board.

Every inch had been plastered with missing cat fliers. There weren't any for missing dogs or any other type of pet, just cats. The flier the sunburned man left promised a cash reward for the safe return of his cat, Puck. According to the flier, Puck was last seen a street over from where Jonas's family lived.

Jonas thought about what he would buy if he claimed the reward money. A new bike, some cool shoes, or a smart phone—something that would impress Danny Martin and his friends, that's what Jonas would buy. Because if he impressed Danny,

Martin, he was sure to get teased less and be liked a little more by the other kids in his class.

His mom's voice interrupted his daydream.

She asked if he'd remembered to pack the medication for Mr. Higgins's cat. Jonas winced. It had slipped his mind amid the excitement. His mother told him he was to drop it off on the way home. Jonas's shoulders fell.

"Ugh—fine!" he groaned.

3
BOCK-BOCK CHICKEN!

Jonas watched some kids climb the jungle gym as he shuffled past George Clinton Elementary. He usually felt nervous any time he saw his school, but without the anxiety of tests, or the anticipation of being teased by his classmates, the building looked ordinary. Jonas wondered if it would look ordinary in three years when he started junior high, or if he would always feel nervous when he saw the school.

He turned onto East North Dusenbury and craned his head at the grand houses that lined the street. Unlike the modest homes in *his* neighborhood, these places boasted exotic architecture and ornately manicured yards. Some had balconies, others featured sprawling porches with built-in gazebos, and few houses even had turrets—rounded towers, like Jonas had seen built into castles.

Jonas often imagined how cool it would be to have a bedroom in the top floor of a turret, with windows all around. He imagined spending his days pretending to be a pirate or even a knight, surveying his domain and watching for advancing armies on the horizon.

Jonas had heard Danny Martin lived on Dusenbury, but wasn't sure in which house. Regardless, he was sure that if Danny did live here, his bedroom was probably in the top of a turret.

Then Jonas came upon the one place on Dusenbury Street in which he, or any kid, would *never* want to live.

A solid wall of gnarled, thorny branches surrounded the property. They rose twice Jonas's height and pressed into the sidewalk, forcing travelers into the grass to avoid injury. But even the overgrown hedgerow couldn't hide the Dusenbury House. It loomed just beyond, like a giant monster poised to strike.

The Dusenbury House was haunted. Everyone in Clintonville knew that. The four-story mansion had been erected ages ago when the neighborhood was farmland. Once the pride of the row, its glory days were firmly behind it. It now sat in ruins, a derelict, haunted by its former owner's tormented ghost.

It was also common knowledge that anything that went over the hedges was lost forever. No one was

willing to step foot onto the property and risk their life for something as measly as a ball or a Frisbee.

Jonas was examining the crumbling manor when his attention was drawn to a third floor window.

The curtains were suddenly yanked aside. He squinted, expecting to see someone through the dirty glass, but there was only darkness. He shielded his eyes from the setting sun and gasped as the tattered fabric fell back into place. Someone—the Dusenbury ghost, most likely—was in there watching him.

Jonas looked around to see if anyone else had witnessed the phenomenon. Passing cars didn't slow and the only other people on the sidewalk was a group of kids riding toward him on bikes.

His fright turned to dread when he heard one of the kids call out, "Bock-bock chicken!" BULLYING

"Oh, no!" he muttered. Jonas tried to walk away, but found his escape blocked as Danny Martin and his friends skidded to a halt, surrounding him.

"Don't you know the Dusenbury House is haunted?" Danny asked. "Do you wanna end up dead in a bucket, Chicken-Boy?"

Danny's friends doubled over their handlebars, laughing.

"I know," Jonas stammered, "I just saw it."

"Saw *what*?" Danny sneered.

"The ghost—up there." Jonas pointed to the

17

window. "The curtain moved back and the ghost looked out at me."

The boys exchanged glances. They couldn't tell if Jonas was joking or if he was serious.

"We gave you too much chicken feed at the party," Danny said. "The sugar's gone straight to your head, Chicken-Boy."

Danny's friends howled.

"I swear, it was right *there*!" Jonas turned again to point to the window. As he did, the schoolbooks under his arm fell, sprawling across the sidewalk. Before he could retrieve them, Danny had bent over his bike and snatched up Jonas's math book.

"Since you know the ghost so well," Danny pitched the book over the hedges, "you won't have a problem getting your book back." Danny and his friends laughed and began to ride off. "That is, unless you're BOCK-BOCK CHICKEN!" he yelled as the gang pedaled away.

Jonas panicked. He looked up at the window. The curtain remained still.

The ghost was probably scared off by the sounds of Danny and his friends, he thought.

He examined the hedgerow and noticed an opening large enough to accommodate a kid about his size. Jonas peeked through the bushes and spotted his textbook hanging on a fallen tree branch in the middle of the yard. He scrambled past the thorns and was pushing through a tall patch of wild grass when a deep creaking sound drew his attention up to the mansion. The front door slowly yawned open, like an ancient mouth, sucking the air of the living into its dusty, decaying lungs. A faint blue light flickered from somewhere deep within the cavernous husk, but Jonas couldn't see anyone there. The door had opened by itself.

He quickly crawled backwards, gathered his remaining schoolbooks, and ran the rest of the way down East North Dusenbury Street.

4
MR. NEIL HIGGINS

The farther away Jonas got from the Dusenbury House, the better he felt. He was worried about how he would explain the loss of his math book, but that seemed like a lot less trouble than being swallowed by a haunted house.

Jonas turned onto <u>East</u> Valleybluff Road. According to the label on the prescription, Mr. Higgins lived nearby.

As he shuffled up the sidewalk, Jonas noticed a cat watching him from a porch.

"Come here, cat!" he called.

The orange tabby eyed him disinterestedly. It thwacked its tail on the banister and turned its half-lidded eyes away.

"Spoiled jerk cat," he whispered.

Jonas trudged up to the porch of 308 East

Valleybluff Road and rang the doorbell. The chimes faded into silence. He knocked, but heard no movement within. He considered leaving the bag in the mailbox, but the toys that littered the porch made Jonas hesitant to leave medicine out with smaller children around.

Just then a jingling sound caught his ear. He followed it around to the back yard, where a grill sat abandoned on a deck.

"And what may I ask are *you* doing?" a voice snapped behind him.

Jonas stood bolt upright. "N-nothing," he stammered. "Honest, I'm just delivering medicine for Mr. Neil Higgins. I'm from Shurmann Veterinary Hospital."

"*I'm* Mr. Neil Higgins," the voice said. "You can leave. And take the medicine with you—I don't want it."

"I'm sorry, but I have to leave the medicine..." Jonas spun around only to find himself alone.

"Down here, child," the voice called.

Jonas's followed the voice down to a one-eyed cat squatted before him.

"You!" he gasped. "You can *talk*?!"

"Not to my knowledge," Neil answered. "At least I've never verbally communicated with a human before. But somehow you can understand me. I noticed it while in the Pinchy Cage earlier today. Tell me," the cat's amber eye studied him, "how do you do it?"

"The _Pinchy Cage_?" Jonas asked.

"Yes, the cage that humans put us in to _pinch_ us with... _instruments_."

"Oh! You mean to give you shots," Jonas said. "It _does_ feel like a pinch. I hate going to the doctor and getting shots too." Jonas paused and looked down at the bag in his hand. "Um, I have to leave this medicine or I'll get in trouble, and..." he inhaled deeply, "...I really need to go home because I think I might be going crazy and I would rather do that in my room. So if you could just tell me where to leave this medication, that would be great."

"Leave it in the mail box by the front door, if you must," Neil said. His ears swiveled back to resemble a pair of velvet horns. "Just, please, be careful where you step. There may be evidence in the yard and I need to examine it before my family returns and tramples it into oblivion."

"Evidence?" Jonas asked. "Evidence of what?"

"You didn't notice all of the fliers for missing cats at the Pinchy Cage?" Neil said as he sniffed the damp soil.

"Of course," Jonas said, "the newest missing flier offered a cash reward for the return of a cat named

Puck." He paused. "Oh! uh, cash is money. People use it to buy—"

"I know what money is," Neil said brusquely. "It doesn't concern me. I'm a cat, if you haven't noticed, and I can't use money. What *does* concern me is what got Cinderella last night."

"Cinderella?" Jonas asked.

"Yes," Neil replied, "one of my neighbors, Cinderella, left our territory in the middle of the night and never returned. My sincere hope is that she was only temporarily run off. She's rather small, and judging from these muddy prints, her pursuer was quite large."

Neil gently pawed at some indentations in a patch of damp soil.

"The man that came into the office yelling about Puck said something was in the neighborhood that shouldn't be here," Jonas said excitedly. "Maybe the prints were made by the same animal."

"Undoubtedly, my boy, undoubtedly. I intend to unmask this villain and find Cinderella and whomever else the tyrant's run off. But I have no use for a cash reward, as I said. However, I *could* offer that handsome reward to someone willing to assist me in my investigation," Neil purred. "Any interested parties should return here at midnight."

"Easy for you to sneak away at midnight," Jonas

scoffed, "you're a cat. You won't get grounded for being caught out past midnight. Cats have it easy. They have people to feed them, to clean up after them, to give them medicine—"

"Then why are they disappearing in the middle of the night if they have it so easy?!" Neil spat. "Cinderella, and many other poor cats, have apparently found big trouble—*much* bigger than getting grounded—and they need help. They need someone brave, who's willing to help those more vulnerable than themselves. They need a hero to find them and I plan on doing everything I can to see that they're safely returned to their families." Neil turned his back to resume his examination and added, "If you know anyone brave, tell them to be here at midnight, because there'll be a cash reward in it for them."

Jonas dropped the bag of medication in the mailbox and sauntered home. He wondered if the conversation he'd had was real or imagined.

It certainly felt real, he thought, *but how in the world is it possible?*

5
CATBOB

Jonas was quiet at dinner. He seemed preoccupied. Mr. and Mrs. Shurmann took turns trying to talk to him, but it was as if he couldn't hear them. And every time they asked him what was wrong, he would mutter, "Nothing." Finally his parents resorted to forced conversation about the Halloween yard displays Mrs. Shurmann had seen on her way home. This was fine by Jonas.

Better they ask me if I'd seen the Halloween Tree on Moors Avenue than ask me too many questions about my day, he thought. Otherwise, Jonas honestly didn't know what he would tell them.

If he told them the truth—that he'd talked to a one-eyed cat—they would worry about him. And maybe they should. Maybe *he* should be worried. But, strangely, Jonas wasn't worried at all. He found that as long as he didn't think about it *too* much, it actually felt pretty normal.

Jonas bit down and discovered his fork was empty. He'd been so consumed by his thoughts he hadn't even noticed he'd cleaned his plate. He pushed his chair back and excused himself from the table.

A couple of hours later, he was in his room, contemplating how to finish his writing homework when his dad knocked.

Mr. Shurmann stood in the doorway wearing a sheepish grin. "So, uh, how did the costume go over at the party?" he asked.

He saw the answer in his son's humorless expression.

He hung his head. "That's what I was afraid of," he sighed. "I'm really sorry, Jonas. I promise: if you put it back in the bag and leave it by the door, I'll take it back tomorrow. Maybe we can still get a soldier or a knight costume at the Halloween store before Beggars' Night begins."

Jonas looked down at his notebook. "It's okay," he said. "A bunch of kids were dressed as soldiers, but no one else was dressed as a chicken. At least my costume was unique."

Although he would have much rather gone as a soldier like Danny Martin and his friends, Jonas wanted to spare his dad's feelings more.

Mr. Shurmann noticed feathers sticking out from under Jonas's shirt collar. "You don't have to live in it, you know."

"I know," Jonas smiled, "but it's warm."

"Okay, just finish your homework and get to bed, okay? Big night tomorrow—trick-or-treat!" he said. "We have to hit a lot of houses, so you'll need your rest. Love you."

"Love you too," Jonas answered.

He listened to his dad lumber down the hall to his room. When he heard the door close, he took out his cell phone and checked the time. Eleven o'clock. Jonas quickly finished his homework, then emptied his book bag on the floor.

He shoved the pile of books and loose papers under his bed and replaced them with a flashlight, a length of rope, a few Halloween candies, and a pocket notebook and pencil. He slipped his coat on and crept quietly into the chilly autumn night.

The neighborhood was deathly quiet. Almost every house Jonas passed lay dark, save for the occasional TV glow in a top floor window. He'd never walked through the neighborhood at this time of night. It was like a different place, a different world. The familiar sounds of children playing, cars driving, and lawn mowers running had been replaced by cryptic songs from insects that hid in the gloom.

Jonas hurried along, making sure to avoid the street lamps. He didn't need any of his neighbors spotting him and calling his parents. And if being out past curfew hadn't made him nervous enough, Jonas began to suspect he was being followed as well.

On two occasions he thought he'd heard a second set of footsteps behind him. When he noticed the peculiar sound, he turned to face his pursuer but found no one there. This creeped him out. Jonas felt like a trespasser in this newly discovered night-world.

A strange noise rattled out of an alley as he passed. He stopped to peer into the shadows but couldn't see anything. He wondered if the sound was made by something he didn't see during the daytime—something the daytime had never seen. A creature that slithered to the surface only under the light of the moon. Maybe it was the same thing that chased off Cinderella. Was it stalking him from the darkness? Jonas's heart pounded. He turned and hurried along.

He reached 308 East Valleybluff Road at exactly midnight. And like most houses at this hour, Neil's house was dark.

Jonas crouched by a parked car and called out as loud as he dared. There was no reply and no sign of

Neil or anyone else. He looked up and down the street before crossing to the opposite row of cars. From there he managed to spot a figure moving along the side of the house. Jonas padded up the walkway and followed it into the shadows.

He reached the gate and spied a thin cat trotting through the back yard toward the alley behind the garage.

"Psst! Do you know where Neil Higgins is? Jonas whispered, "Hang on a second!"

He jogged through the yard, but found the alley deserted. He looked around the garbage and recycling bins and called out, but remembered the tabby that ignored him earlier that afternoon.

It's no use, he thought. *I should have known. Cats just ignore people.*

Jonas took a last look around then turned for home when a voice behind him said, "Good, good! You decided to come, after all."

Jonas spun around, but still didn't see anyone. "Don't tell me you can turn invisible too," he whispered.

"Of course not, boy," the voice answered. "If I could, there would be no reason to partner with a human."

He followed the voice to where Neil Higgins sat perched on the edge of a garage roof beside a sleepy-faced, peach-colored cat. Jonas recognized the new feline as the cat he'd followed into the alley. Its tail was abnormally short with a crooked end, suggesting an accident—or predator—had claimed the missing half.

"This is my partner in investigation, CatBob," Neil said. "CatBob, I'd like you to meet, er, what *is* your name, anyway? I don't believe formal introductions were made."

"I'm Jonas," he whispered. "Jonas Shurmann."

"Pleasure to make your acquaintance, Jonas Shurmann," CatBob purred. The feline leaned over the edge and pushed its cheeks forward to form an unmistakable smile. It was then that Jonas recognized the cat.

"Hey, I know you!" he exclaimed.

"Oh, of course you do," Neil spat sarcastically. "Doesn't everyone?" His ears were flattened with annoyance as he watched CatBob hop down onto a tall fence and leap into Jonas's arms.

Jonas remembered meeting CatBob about a year ago when he had been playing with some kids on East Valleybluff Road.

"I thought your tail looked familiar," he said. "Yeah, you're the cat that always ran out to say hello."

Although Jonas didn't know his name at the time,

CatBob had distinguished himself from the other neighborhood felines by greeting every person that walked down East Valleybluff Road—including Jonas. CatBob was the most social cat Jonas had ever met. All summer, Jonas made a point to visit him every time he rode down Valleybluff on his bike. That was before he started working at the vet's office; before cats began to annoy him.

"So, you two solve crimes?" Jonas asked as he cradled CatBob in his arms. The peach feline pressed his body to Jonas and rumbled with contentment.

"Yes," Neil answered, "but only cat-specific cases."

"What kinds of cases can cats investigate?" Jonas asked.

"Stolen toys, stolen kills, and territory disputes— the usual stuff. But this wave of disappearances is more than CatBob and I can handle alone," Neil added. "To get to the bottom of this mystery, we must venture outside of our territory, and there are... *things* out there that could...*get* us."

"*Get* you?" Jonas asked.

"Yes, *get* us!" Neil exclaimed. "Being *got* is every cat's greatest fear. We have to be suspicious of everything. I check under every leaf, every shoe, anything a predator could possibly hide in *or* under. Because it only takes *once* for something to strike while your guard's down and—*MEOW!*" Neil let out shrill caterwaul.

"Shhh!" Jonas hissed. "You're going to wake the whole neighborhood!"

"It *gets* you," Neil spat, "and that's the end of your ride! No more treats, no more belly rubs, no more mice, no more lying in the sunshine..."

"No more eye," CatBob added grimly.

Jonas couldn't tell if Neil had heard his friend. The gray feline sat silent, staring into the darkness.

"Is that what happened to your eye?" Jonas asked.

"It's my reminder that bad things, can, and do, happen no matter how good we are," Neil muttered.

"I'm sorry, I had no idea. So, what kinds of things are out there—that could get you, I mean," Jonas asked, remembering his own suspicion that something had followed him to Neil's house.

"Many things pose dangers to cats," Neil said as he straightened up. "Foxes, big, smelly dogs, raccoons, cars, and now whatever's taking cats in the middle of the night. That's why we need human assistance. Most animals are afraid of humans, but they aren't afraid of cats," he explained. "We felines have to be careful because we're the most vulnerable of all human companions. Only mice, birds, and squirrels are afraid of us."

"Lots of people keep mice and birds as pets," Jonas said.

"Don't be ridiculous, Jonas. Everyone knows they're just food," Neil snorted. "Anyway, in exchange for your assistance, you're welcome to any reward money offered by the families of the missing cats."

Jonas gently lowered CatBob to the ground. The peach cat nimbly hopped atop some discarded boxes and then onto a recycling bin.

"Okay," Jonas said, "so, who are we looking for?"

"Her name is Cinderella," said CatBob. "She's a small, black, bobtailed cat. She and her brother Pierre live with me, but Pierre's too old and frail to help with the search, so it's up to us."

"So, where do we start?" Jonas asked.

The cats turned their heads in reply. Jonas followed their gaze east to where the alley intersected with the next street.

"There," Neil said, "beyond our territory. That's where Puck was last seen."

6
WEIRD PRINTS

Jonas waited until there were no headlights visible from either direction of Moors Avenue. Then he carefully shepherded his new partners across into the unknown territory.

The two felines sniffed everything they encountered. Neil, paranoid about being *got*, cautiously tapped every other leaf in his path.

This made Jonas nervous. They were too visible at this intersection to linger.

"I know this is a new place," he whispered, "but we have to move faster, guys. If any adults see me, they'll call my parents and then I won't be able to help you anymore."

"But we have to," said CatBob. "It's our nature. Anytime cats encounter new territory we have to explore every inch. We're natural investigators because of our need to know the lay of the land. We may not be as big and strong as dogs, but we're smarter," he added. "Dogs have no choice but to risk death or injury in a confrontation. Cats, on the other paw, seek the quickest path to the highest ground. That way we're out of a predator's reach and can wait them out."

Jonas never realized cats faced so many dangers on a daily basis. He'd assumed any place humans lived was safe for cats. But now that he was experiencing the neighborhood from the perspective of his two new friends, he realized his assumption was wrong.

The trio plodded along until the two felines suddenly stopped and declared, "This is it!"

They were standing before a white house that looked identical to most on the street.

"How do you know this is the place?" Jonas asked.

"You can't smell them?" Neil said as he swept the ground with his tail. "The cat and that...*stink*."

"I'll bet those weird prints are all over this yard," CatBob said. "Whatever it is, it smells desperate and hungry."

Jonas fished his flashlight from his book bag and played the beam over the yard. Within a few moments he saw them; deep indentations just like the ones

Neil had shown him that afternoon. He checked the address. It matched the one on Puck's "missing" flier.

"You're right!" Jonas said. "It—whatever *it* is— was definitely here. But what are we looking for, exactly?"

"Clues, if there *are* any," Neil said. "What exactly, I'm not sure. Just look for anything that's out of place."

Jonas noticed CatBob was standing with his back arched and his ears flat to his head.

"What's wrong, CatBob?" he asked, but the peachy feline didn't reply. He just continued stalking toward a mess of boxwood bushes growing against the house.

Neil ran to Jonas's side. "That had better not be a dog," he whispered.

Jonas threw the beam onto the bushes but couldn't see anything. CatBob crouched, ready to pounce when a startling shriek rang out.

A black figure shot from the boxwoods and vanished into the darkness. CatBob gave chase, plunging headlong into the unknown.

7
A FRIEND

Jonas and Neil ran blindly after CatBob, with neither knowing in which direction he had run. Jonas shined the flashlight beam around while Neil scanned the street with his low-light vision. They spotted a clowder of cats huddled under a porch light a few doors down, and among the felines was their peach-colored comrade.

As they approached the house, Neil whispered to Jonas, "Don't look anyone in the eye."

Before Jonas could ask why, a commotion arose on the porch.

"He tried to get me!" howled a long-haired black cat.

"You were spying on my friends and me," CatBob retorted. "You startled us! We thought you were the thing that ran Puck off."

"*Why*, is it here?!" The black cat's eyes grew large with alarm. "Where? Don't let it get me!"

She hopped up on a rocking chair and looked wildly about the yard. When she spotted Jonas and Neil, she yowled and arched her back. The other cats turned and readied themselves to run.

"It's quite all right," Neil purred. "Please, try to keep your composure, friends. We're detectives investigating the disappearance of your neighbor, Puck."

The cats' attention wandered from the squat cyclopean detective up to Jonas, who immediately averted his eyes from the porch.

"This is our human associate, Jonas Shurmann," Neil continued as he climbed the steps to the porch. "And I believe you've all met my partner in investigation, CatBob. We were searching Puck's yard for clues when your friend here suddenly abandoned her hiding spot in the bushes."

Jonas grabbed the notebook and pencil out of his book bag and wrote down the address. He then set to work jotting down descriptions of the cats, making sure not to look any of them in the eye as he did.

He first noted the fuzzy, long-haired black cat in the rocking chair, then a lean cat with black and white cow markings, a gray cat with a strikingly plush coat, an orange tabby that was as wide as he was tall, and was tall, and finally, Jonas eyed the oldest cat he'd ever seen.

The feline's gaunt frame had a uniquely angular appearance that only age can bestow. Its oily coat separated into chunks that tangled into hard, flat mats. But the cat's face testified most to its years. Brown spots had formed around its nose and under its weepy eyes, giving the appearance that rust had begun to take hold. This collection of morbid features gave the beholder the impression that the cat had somehow lived beyond its own death.

"Why you wastin' your time lookin' for Puck?" Jonas heard the orange tabby grumble. "More food in our bowl since that bow-legged moocher left. Good riddance, I say!"

The other cats mumbled in agreement. Jonas recorded the statement and reactions.

"So, you were an acquaintance of the missing feline?" CatBob asked the tabby. "And what is your name?"

"I'm Gary," the big cat answered.

"Gary's right," added the cow cat. "Puck ate our food all the time, and I don't recall ever inviting him."

"And you are?" Neil asked.

"Tom," he answered. "This is Oso, our neighbor from across the street," he nodded to the plush gray cat. He then directed attention to the ancient feline Jonas had been studying. "The old-timer is Baby and the scaredy-cat on the chair is Boo-Boo."

"Scaredy-cat, indeed!" Boo-Boo hissed as she swiveled her ears back and thwacked her bushy tail. "Where were you when that thing got Puck? Courageously holding down a food dish on a brightly lit porch, that's where. For shame, Thomas!"

"So, you actually *saw* this thing?" Jonas asked as he finished scribbling down the black cat's statement.

The porch fell silent. The cats folded their ears back and tensed their muscles in anticipation of flight.

"The human, he— How can he—?" Boo-Boo stammered as the hackles rose on her back.

Sensing their investigation was in danger of collapse, CatBob stepped in front of Jonas and addressed the clowder.

"It's true, the human can understand cats and is somehow able communicate with us as well."

"He'll get us—he'll *get* us *all!*" Boo-Boo yowled. She leapt onto the crest rail of the chair as the others began to whine and hiss.

"He isn't going to *get* anyone!" Neil announced. "This boy has volunteered to help us find the missing cats. Surely you've heard about the villain preying upon our brothers and sisters. This boy is here to help us find out what's become of our fellow felines. Where are *your* humans right now? Are they out looking for the missing cats, or are they in their beds, sleeping?"

The clowder became silent. They looked at Jonas, who stayed focused on Neil.

CatBob stepped in. "We don't know how he can do what he does—I don't think he knows—but we're lucky to have a human who cares enough to help us. A member of *my* family, Cinderella, went missing two nights ago. Our yard was covered in large tracks just like Puck's, so if anyone saw anything last night, we'd like to hear about it." CatBob looked over the felines one by one then added, "Because as far as we can tell, the thing getting cats *isn't* human. Regardless, we intend to stop it."

The cats remained silent as their collective gaze drifted from the two feline detectives up to Jonas. The lull was broken by a voice hardened from decades of midnight caterwauling.

"Oso and Gary saw it," croaked the ancient feline.

The accused cats slunk backwards, mumbling apologies for Baby's senility until their escape was cut off by the elder feline.

"Tell them!" he demanded. "Tell them why I

found you two huddled together on the porch, trembling like newborn kittens that morning."

Oso and Gary thwacked their tails in silent defiance until the other cats crowded in on them, hissing.

"Okay, okay! We were out here two nights ago when we heard a yowl comin' from Puck's place," Gary admitted. "We thought he was squarin' off with another cat, but then we heard some strange sounds and we knew it wasn't no cat he was fightin'."

"And it didn't sound like any dog I've ever heard before," Oso added. "It was some kind of big, scary..."

"Beast?" Boo-Boo squealed.

"I guess so," Gary grunted, "but we didn't see nothin', I swear. We..." he hung his head, "...we was too scared to get close enough to get a look at it."

"We went to Puck's house after daybreak and saw the strange prints in the yard," Oso said. "Right then, we knew it was more than our imaginations running wild."

"Good heavens! Why didn't you say something?" Tom asked.

"Puck was always eating our food," Gary stammered, "he—"

"You mean *our* food, don't you, you big fuzzy pumpkin?" Baby scolded. "You two don't live here either. You have no right to accuse Puck of being a moocher when both of you are guilty of the exact same thing."

"But it's different—" the pair protested.

"Dogwash!" Baby cried. "Puck might have taken some getting used to, but he was no different than any other cat that tires of the solitude of his territory and longs for some feline camaraderie."

The sound of approaching footfalls broke the tension. Jonas stopped scribbling in his notebook, grabbed his book bag, and dove behind a tall thicket of bushes. The cats leapt off the porch and trotted merrily down the walkway to greet the approaching visitor.

"Good evening, Tom!" Jonas heard a man's voice say. "Come on, Gary, be nice, big boy. There you go. Hey there, Boo-Boo. Aren't you a pretty girl! Look at you, Baby! Still so spry for an old-timer. Hello, Oso! How's my plush boy?"

The fuzzy hoard surrounded the visitor, vying for pets, scritches, and belly rubs. Then Jonas heard a sudden note of surprise in the man's voice.

"Is that *you*, CatBob?! What are you and Neil doing all the way over *here*—especially at this hour?! Are you boys lost, or did I just interrupt some wild cat party? You might've had too much catnip to drive, so what do you say I walk you boys home? Come on."

Jonas listened to the footfalls fade into the distance as the cats returned to the porch, purring with satisfaction. Jonas counted all but CatBob and Neil. He peered out from behind the bushes but saw no one on the street. He asked the cats who the visitor was.

"A friend," they chimed.

Jonas thanked them for their help and headed home, wondering just who CatBob and Neil's friend was.

On his way back, Jonas again felt as though he was being followed. Strange sounds crept from between houses as he passed, spurring him to quicken his pace. As he reached East Thurber Road, he distinctly heard footfalls behind him.

Jonas bolted into the alley that cut behind his house, rounded the garage, and crashed into the back door, where he frantically struggled to free the key from his pants pocket. When he finally did, he found his trembling fingers unable to guide the key into the lock.

The crunch of dried leaves alerted him to a presence approaching from behind. He spun around to find the yard vacant, except for the few abandoned toys lying buried under the blanket of leaves. But it was something Jonas couldn't see—something he sensed, just beyond the porch light's reach—that caused him to redouble his efforts to open the door.

After a few frantic attempts, his shaking hands finally managed to guide the key home. He twisted the knob and slipped into the quiet warmth of the house.

Jonas snapped the deadbolt back into place and peered out the window. The porch light flickered off. Something in the gloom moved and a pair of yellow eyes appeared at the edge of the yard. Jonas watched them hover for a few moments.

Then he blinked, and they were gone.

8
CHICKEN POWER

While working at his mom's office the next afternoon, Jonas noticed two new fliers had been added to the bulletin board: one for CatBob and Neil's friend Cinderella, and another for a cat named Tiger.

Jonas took all the fliers down and sorted them by date, then ran them through the photocopier. He stuffed the warm stack of fresh copies in his book bag and reposted the originals. Jonas hoped organizing the fliers might help people recognize the cats more easily. When he'd finished, he noticed the receptionist and one of the vet techs watching him.

"Nice job, Jonas!" they said.

He forced a smile but didn't feel like his efforts deserved praise. So far, he and his friends had failed to find the missing cats.

* * *

Jonas went straight to the garage when he got home where he set to work pinning a map of Clintonville to the wall. Once it was up, he pinned his "missing" fliers around the map in chronological order. Then, he connected each flier to the "last seen" location on the map with string and push pins.

He'd gotten the idea from his mother's favorite police show on TV. Jonas knew if he and his partners were going to find the missing cats and claim the reward money, they had better get serious. And since all real detectives had offices, he figured the garage would be theirs. It was a little messy, and smelled like dust and oil, but it was about as private as they were going to get.

Jonas stood back and looked at the map. He noticed the push pins formed a rough circular pattern with East North Dusenbury Street running horizontally through the middle.

He fetched a red marker from his book bag and held it out so the edge ran vertically down the middle of the circle. He slowly walked forward, keeping his eye fixed on the spot where the marker's edge and Dusenbury Street intersected. When he reached the map, he circled it. Jonas gasped and dropped the marker. He knew exactly what sat in the middle of the red circle he had just drawn: the Dusenbury House!

Maybe the thing that watched me from the window is Beast's owner, Jonas thought. *Or maybe...*

Something scratched at the door.

Jonas froze. There it was again. Was it the thing that followed him last night? Had it been waiting in the alley for him? Jonas looked around and grabbed a rake from the wall. He held his breath and yanked the door open. CatBob and Neil spilled into the garage, greeting him with tail-hugs and meows. Jonas heaved a sigh of relief and then began explaining his discovery to his partners.

The cats perched atop his dad's workbench and listened as he presented his findings with giddy shouts and wild gestures. When Jonas revealed his conclusion that the Dusenbury House was somehow at the center of this mystery, he paused, expecting the cats to react to this revelation, but the two felines remained silent.

"You guys don't think this is a big deal? Look, the Dusenbury House definitely has something to do with these disappearances," he said. "I don't know exactly what I saw the other night, but someone—or some*thing*—is definitely living in there."

His friends watched him but said nothing.

"Are you guys angry that I allowed your friend to take you home last night?" Jonas asked. "And speaking of this *friend* of yours, who is he?"

He waited for an answer that didn't come.

Sweat beaded on his forehead. Jonas was frustrated that his friends were ignoring him.

"What did I *do*, guys?" he pleaded. "I had to hide. I couldn't be caught out after curfew. If someone would've called my parents, I'd have been grounded for the next two years."

Jonas wiped his forehead and wondered how the three of them would cope with the summer heat in the garage. It was a cool day, but even without his—

Jonas stopped. He told the cats to stay put and ran out the door.

The two felines exchanged expressions of concern but didn't move. A few minutes later the sound of galloping sneakers was followed by Jonas crashing through the door in his costume.

"The Dusenbury House is at the center of these disappearances!" he exclaimed.

CatBob and Neil gasped.

"How do you know this?" Neil asked.

But instead of answering him, Jonas began to laugh maniacally. CatBob hopped down from the workbench and approached his friend, who was doubled over on the floor in hysterics.

"What on earth is the matter, Jonas?" CatBob asked. "You're acting strangely. Did something happen?"

"This ridiculous-looking costume," Jonas cackled, wiping tears from his eyes. "That's how I do it!"

"How you do *what*, my boy?" Neil asked.

"How I talk to you guys," Jonas gasped. "My dad got it for me for Halloween, but the kids in my class laughed at it, so I hated it. But it must be magic."

"Then why are you laughing?" CatBob asked.

"Because," Jonas giggled, "if someone was going to make a magic costume that gave you the power to talk to cats, shouldn't it be a cat costume? Why would they make it a chicken costume? Wouldn't cats try to eat you?" Jonas laid on the floor cracking up until his stomach muscles began to cramp.

CatBob climbed onto his chest. "We don't want to eat you, Jonas," the peachy feline said. "We're worried about you. You aren't making any sense."

"Where did your father acquire that costume?" Neil asked.

"I don't know," Jonas answered. "He said he bought it from an old lady at an antique mall."

"Well, hang on to it," Neil said. "At least until we get to the bottom of this mystery." The gray cat studied Jonas's map. "So, how did you come to the conclusion that the Dusenbury House has a part in all this?"

Jonas heard his father call before he could

answer.

"I forgot, it's Beggars' Night!" he said as he wiped his eyes and dusted off his costume. "I have to go, guys. Meet me back here after the streets empty out. We have a new case."

Jonas pointed to the newest "missing" flier—the one for Tiger.

9
BEGGARS' NIGHT

Dusk brought hordes of children capering through the streets with only one thing on their minds—candy. But Jonas Shurmann wasn't one of them. He was too preoccupied with his thoughts to do any capering. In fact, if his dad hadn't directed him up each walkway, Jonas wouldn't have managed to trick-or-treat a single house.

And while Mr. Shurmann usually shared Jonas's excitement for Halloween, this time he found himself instead sharing his son's downcast mood. He was convinced that he had ruined Jonas's Halloween by making him wear the chicken costume. And this belief was reinforced when he spied a few kids pointing at Jonas and snickering secretively to one another. But Jonas was lost in his own world. He shuffled along unaware of their quiet ridicule—but

Mr. Shurmann noticed, and it *did* affect him.

Jonas's mom attempted to dispel her husband's black cloud by commenting on how adorable she thought the costume was and punctuating every compliment Jonas received with a "See, I told ya'." But nothing seemed to help. Mr. Shurmann's brows remained knitted.

Despite his father's assumptions, the truth was Jonas was too absorbed in other matters to even realize Beggars' Night was happening. His thoughts were haunted by the image of the red circle on the map.

He knew for a fact that the Dusenbury House was haunted, but what other terrible secrets lurked within its decaying walls? Was something coming out at night to stalk the streets of Clintonville, and if so, what was it?

A bump on the head brought Jonas back to the outside world. He'd walked right into a man who was standing with his daughter on the sidewalk. Mrs. Shurmann pulled Jonas back and apologized to the man. Jonas's cheeks were flushed with embarrassment.

He looked around and realized they were stuck in a Halloween traffic jam. He climbed onto a retaining wall to see if he could spot the source of the hold up. The line began at CatBob's and Neil's houses where a group of adults stood around chatting and casually passing out candy.

Jonas hopped down and looked in his bag. Judging from the amount of candy he was carrying, they must've been trick-or-treating for a while, but he'd been too wrapped up in his thoughts to know how far, or for how long, his family had been walking.

Eventually, the line began to move again and Jonas shuffled up the walkway among a troupe of other costumed kids. After thanking the woman for his treat, Jonas spied a group of kids huddled together in the yard and decided to investigate.

He wandered over and discovered CatBob, sprawled in the grass. The peach feline laid with his eyes closed and a smile on his snout. The kids took turns gently stroking his soft coat and whispering his name. Jonas could hear him purring from where he stood. He decided to leave the feline celebrity to his adoring fans and marched up the next walkway where he found the man who had picked up Neil at the vet's office. The man greeted Jonas with the same bright smile.

"Trick-or-treat!" Jonas called.

"Hey, cool costume!" the man said. "You don't see many like that anymore."

"Thanks," Jonas mumbled. "And thanks for the candy."

The man waved to Jonas's mom and yelled, "Happy Halloween!"

That's when Jonas noticed a surly face on the other side of the glass storm door. Neil Higgins sat glowering at the children fawning over CatBob. His ears pointed out like velvet horns.

"That's Neil," the man said to Jonas.

"Yeah, I remember him from the vet's office."

"He's jealous of CatBob over there getting petted by all of those kids," the man chuckled. "He's in a pretty rotten mood."

Neil looked up at Jonas, but didn't say anything. He just went back to being disgusted by the display of adoration for his friend.

Jonas walked back to his parents wearing a grin.

"Well, look who's back with us!" his dad announced. "Are you maybe, finally ready to do some trick-or-treating? Maybe, do you think?"

"What are you talking about?" Jonas rolled his eyes at his dad's lame act. "You're lucky this bag's heavy enough to slow me down. Otherwise you wouldn't be able to keep up. Come on, we've got a lot of houses to hit—remember?"

As they worked their way toward Moors Avenue, it was agreed that they should to try to cover at least one side of East North Dusenbury Street before it was all over, because the big houses would probably give big candy bars.

They snapped some pictures in front of the Halloween Tree at Nightshade Road then continued wading through the throngs of costumed revelers who apparently had the same idea.

As they snaked their way through a group of kids in soldier's fatigues, Jonas heard someone yell, "Bock-bock Chicken!" Mocking laughter followed. Mr. Shurmann squeezed Jonas's hand like a vice.

"Ow, Dad!" he yelped.

"Sorry." Mr. Shurmann bent down. "You okay? I didn't mean to. It just makes me mad—"

"Obviously. You almost crushed my hand."

"I'm really sorry about the costume—"

"It's okay, Dad," Jonas said. "It's not your fault Danny Martin's a jerk."

Mr. Shurmann rose to his feet and nodded. The wrinkles on his forehead smoothed. "You're right, Jonas," he said, nodding. "You're right! Let's go get some candy."

As soon as they turned the corner, Jonas let go of his dad's hand and bolted up the first walkway. Not only were the houses much larger on Dusenbury Street, but so were the yards. Unlike the homes in Jonas's immediate neighborhood, the places on Dusenbury sat far back from the sidewalk, so Jonas had to run up the walkways to keep the pace.

After the third house Jonas was getting sweaty under his feathers, but he found his chicken feet weren't nearly as difficult to run in as he'd anticipated. In fact, he made impressive time and the extra effort paid off. At the end of each sprint he was rewarded with a large treat. They'd covered half of the south side of the street before crossing to the north with only minutes remaining.

By nine o'clock, porch lights were going dark and the crowds began to thin.

"Time to head back," his dad said, "but it looks like you made out like a robber baron, Jonas! Do you need me to carry your bag for you?"

"No, thanks," Jonas said. "I've got it."

Although the bag was pretty heavy, Jonas was much too proud of his haul to allow someone else the prestige of lugging it back to the house.

"Watch out—thorns!" Mr. Shurmann called as he shoved Jonas off the sidewalk and into the grass.

Jonas stumbled and turned to see the Dusenbury House looming over the hedges he had nearly walked into. He'd overheard adults call the bushes an eye sore, but Jonas was thankful for them. He saw the hedgerow as the only thing preventing the dark mansion from escaping its lot and unleashing its untold evils upon the whole city.

Jonas's dad saw the trepidation in his expression

and laughed.

"What's wrong, Bub?" he asked. "I bet no one's been brave enough to knock on the door of the Dusenbury House all night. Imagine what the person that lives there would give the kid brave enough to do it. Probably a sports car or a private jet or something."

Jonas's mom chuckled and rolled her eyes at Mr. Shurmann, but Jonas wasn't paying any attention. His gaze was locked on the third-floor window, where he'd seen the curtains move.

He gasped when he saw something yank the curtains back just as before. But this time Jonas could see what was moving them—human bones!

A skeletal hand had swept the fabric aside then pressed itself against the dirty glass, followed by a skull. Jonas could feel its deathly gaze clutching at his heart as it pounded wildly in his chest. He dropped his candy bag and ran screaming down the sidewalk.

When Jonas's parents finally caught up with him, he refused to tell them what he'd seen. He knew they wouldn't believe him. He knew that without proof, no one would believe anything he said about the house, the skeleton, the cats, or any of it. He just mumbled something about the house giving him the creeps and they walked home in silence.

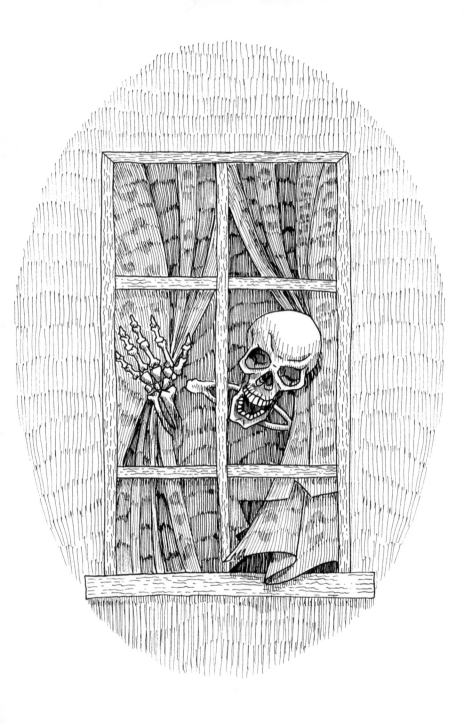

10

BLACKJACK

Beggars' Night was over. All the vampires, witches, superheroes, and princesses had retreated to their homes to enjoy the night's spoils, leaving the Chicken-Boy and his two cat companions to haunt the streets alone.

The trio had turned onto East Newcomb Road when CatBob and Neil suddenly stopped. Their ears and tails stood at attention.

"What is it?" Jonas asked, but neither cat answered.

The felines crouched low and peered across to the south side of the street. Leaves rustled. Jonas's partners jerked their heads back and forth in unison. But Jonas couldn't see the invisible phantom they were following through the gloom.

Then, after a few silent moments, he saw a black

streak flash through a street lamp beam and vanish again behind a bush.

Leaves stirred behind the detectives. They turned to discover a plump, mackerel-striped cat stalking through the murk, closely followed by a leaner, marble-coated companion. CatBob tensed, anticipating a confrontation, but as he watched the pair, it became apparent they were hunting the phantom he and his friends had been watching.

The newcomers sniffed the air and eyed a thicket of bushes across the street.

A slender black tail unfurled from out of the shrubs like a wisp of smoke. Two yellow eyes blinked open in the darkness.

"Blaaack—jaaack," the marble-coated feline sang mockingly, "we see you! You can't hide from us. Eventually you'll get tired of running and then we'll get you.

"And your walkway will be mine!" the mackerel-striped cat added. "I'm going to rub my teeth all over those steps and then I'm going to roll up and down that walkway, because it'll be all *mine*."

"No! No! No! It's mine!" The phantom cried as it shot from the bushes and was joined by the newcomers.

"Bullies!" Neil grumbled. "This Blackjack is probably the smallest cat on the block, so she's become an easy target for these insecure cats who try to prove their strength by terrorizing her." He smacked his tail on the ground in disgust. "There's no excuse for such behavior from full-grown cats."

"Agreed," CatBob said as he readied to pounce.

Jonas and Neil watched as the black streak darted by, closely pursued by its two tormentors. CatBob leapt onto the lean marble-coated cat and pinned him to the ground. He hissed and squirmed, but Cat-Bob's paws held him fast.

"Hey! What's the big idea?!" the mackerel-striped cat shouted. "Get off of Baba. He wasn't bothering you."

"Oh, I'm sorry," CatBob smiled, "is this not fun for you? You two make bullying look like such a good time, I wanted to try it myself."

"Ha-ha! This isn't any of your business," Baba sneered. "This is *our* territory. What are *you* even doing here?"

"We've come to learn what we can about Tiger's disappearance," Neil said.

"You'll have to talk to the fraidy-cat," the mackerel-striped cat said, "if you can catch her."

"I'm Blackjack," the phantom called from the dark, "and Tiger was my brother. What do you want to know?"

CatBob released Baba and scanned the shadows

for the yellow eyes.

"We want to know how he disappeared and when," Jonas answered.

"The boy—!" Baba gasped.

"Oh, yeah, our human can talk to cats," CatBob chimed, "so don't bother trying to play cute. He knows what you're up to."

Jonas spotted the golden eyes blink open again.

"Last night, we followed the scent of chicken out of our territory," Blackjack said. "Our family feeds us, but what cat can pass up fresh bird?"

Neil watched the streak move in short bursts, stopping only when hidden from view. "She's really fast," he breathed to his partner.

CatBob nodded in agreement. "She's fast, all right, but not untouchable."

"The scent led to an old house a few blocks away," Blackjack continued. "It's surrounded by thorny bushes with only one opening to the yard, but..."

CatBob crouched low and wiggled his butt.

"...every cat knows to stay away from that house, so we decided to turn back. That's when something leapt from the bushes and began chasing us."

CatBob fixed on the streak as it approached.

"It forced Tiger through the opening," Blackjack said in a strained voice. "I wanted to help him, but I couldn't make myself enter that yard. There was something—"

CatBob sprang. His paws made contact, pinning Blackjack in the grass. "Gotcha!" he shouted.

Her body trembled under its velveteen coat. Large, golden eyes shimmered up at him, pleading for mercy.

"Enough running! You're making me dizzy." he said as he released her. "These two aren't going to try anything while we're here." He nodded toward her pursuers.

"Luna and Baba are my friends," Blackjack said weakly. "We were just...playing a game."

Jonas shook his head. Blackjack was reciting the same excuse he'd given his teacher when Danny and the other kids had bullied him. This made Jonas realize he'd not only been lying to his teachers, but to himself as well.

"No, they're not playing, Blackjack, they're bullying you," Jonas said, "because they think physical strength is the only thing that makes someone strong or brave. But they're not even brave or strong enough to help you find Tiger." He looked over at Baba and Luna who sat with their heads hung.

"I don't think there's any help for Tiger," Blackjack wailed. "He's gone, and it's all my fault. I wasn't brave enough to save him." She shuddered with grief. "I let him down. That thing should have gotten me instead."

Jonas's heart ached for her. He knew what it was like to feel helpless. He crouched next to the inky feline and gently stroked her back.

"Well, you don't have to be brave alone," he said. "My name is Jonas Shurmann and these are my friends, CatBob and Neil Higgins. We're detectives, and we're going to find Tiger and all of the other missing cats, aren't we, guys?"

His partners nodded.

Neil turned to Baba and Luna. "Have either one of you seen this beast Blackjack described?"

"Sure," Luna said, "it's a big, terrible-looking creature with huge paws and dripping jaws, that looks just like..." she arched her back and began hissing loudly.

"...like *that*!" she spat.

Everyone turned to see a large figure stagger out of a nearby alley.

At first, Jonas thought it was a huge dog, but it looked different than any dog he'd ever seen. It was skinny and haggard and there was something wild about it.

A guttural growl rumbled from its jaws, sending chills down Jonas's spine.

"Run for your hides! It's going to *get* us all!" Luna cried as she, Baba, and Blackjack, all took off in different directions.

Neil pressed against Jonas and hugged him with his tail. "Don't let it *get* me!" the gray cat whispered.

The creature eyed the trio for a few moments before turning back into the alley. CatBob trotted after it with Neil and Jonas tagging behind.

11
THE BEAST

The detectives exchanged whispered observations as they crept along, but couldn't agree on *what* exactly they were following. Only one thing was obvious to everyone: the Beast—whatever it was—was big and dangerous.

They trailed the creature as it wandered from one garbage bin to another, scavenging for food. Then it darted around a bend in the alley and was lost from view.

The three friends ran to the bend and took cover behind a garage. The cats' ears scanned for any sound of movement, but all was quiet.

Jonas fished a flashlight from his book bag and inched to the corner. He glanced around the wall. There was no sign of the Beast.

The trio rounded the bend into a dead-end flanked

by four garages. Tall heaps of building materials, car parts, and discarded furniture barricaded the doors. The broken asphalt ended at a guardrail that bore a No Outlet sign. Weeds grew taller than Jonas for twenty feet beyond before giving way to a slim path that snaked into a wooded ravine.

"It might have run into the woods," Jonas whispered. He shone the beam through the weeds but found no trace of its passage. Likewise the junk heaps yielded no scent for his partners.

"It has to be here," CatBob said. "Something that big and ugly doesn't just disappear."

A growl rumbled out of the darkness. CatBob and Neil crouched and spat panicked hisses toward the guardrail.

Jonas backed over to them. "Get in the bag, guys," he whispered. He slid the book bag off his shoulder and dropped his flashlight in. He had just placed Neil inside when the Beast came staggering out of the weeds.

The creature's black lips peeled back to reveal a grin of white daggers. Another gut-rattling growl boomed through the alley and sent Jonas and CatBob scrambling around the corner.

The alley ahead stretched for a half mile to High Street and Jonas knew there was no way they could outrun the monster. Their only chance of surviving would be to hide—and quickly. But where?

Without breaking his stride, Jonas scooped up CatBob, scaled a pile of refuse and hopped a fence before pausing to dump his furry friend in the book bag with Neil.

The cats peeked out of the zipper in time to see the Beast clear the fence and charge toward them.

"He's gaining ground!" CatBob yelled.

Jonas didn't answer. He turned and dashed through the yard of a large brick house.

He raced along the narrow walkway when a door swung open in front of him. Jonas sidestepped in time to avoid being pinned against the tall fence that ran the length of the yard.

"Whoa!" a man shouted from the doorway. "Careful, kid, I almost squashed you!"

"Sorry, Mister!" Jonas panted as he reached the back yard. He was headed toward the alley when he heard the man yell again, followed by loud barking.

He turned to see the man braced against the door as it shook under a flurry of savage blows.

"Hey, kid!" the man yelled. "If this is your psycho dog, tell it to stop!"

As if by command, the attack suddenly stopped. After waiting a few seconds, the man cautiously swung the door closed.

The Beast was gone.

As Jonas stumbled into the alley, he realized he was almost home. If he could manage to run just a block farther they could reach his house, or at least the garage. Unfortunately a stitch in his side forced him to stop a few strides into the trek.

He doubled over and clutched his gut. Running with his friends on his back was exhausting. The weight in his book bag shifted and squirmed. Muffled protests poured from the zipper.

"Sorry, guys," Jonas coughed, "I just need a second."

That's when a commotion erupted ahead.

Half a block up, he spotted a pack of dogs swarming a wooden deck. They ran in circles, barking a chorus at something hidden behind the neighbor's fence. Then the dogs suddenly bolted down the length of the yard. When they reached the alley fence line, a large figure leapt over the neighboring fence, turned, and charged toward Jonas.

Jonas took off down a back street that emptied into East Thurber Road with the Beast right behind him.

Neil peeked out. The monster was closing the gap with every graceful stride.

"Find the high ground!" Neil cried. "Climb, Jonas, quickly, before it gets us!"

That's when Jonas remembered what CatBob had

told him about cats not being as strong as dogs. He'd said they avoid confrontation by seeking the highest ground.

That's it! The highest ground, thought Jonas, *but where?*

A car swung into the alley and swerved, barely missing Jonas. Jonas skirted the car and cut down the alleyway that ran parallel to Thurber. Behind him, the car's engine revved and the horn honked.

Jonas glanced over his shoulder and saw the Beast in the car's headlights. It hesitated for a few moments then tore around the vehicle to follow him down the alley. Jonas charged ahead as the high ground came into view.

"Hang on, guys!" he yelled as he broke into a final, desperate sprint.

He leapt into the air and grasped wildly at their one chance of escape. Cold metal bit his palms as he seized the middle rung of an aluminum ladder and scrambled frantically upward. He reached the roof of an old conversion van and paused.

Behind him, the sound of scattering gravel grew louder, then a crash resounded through the alley. The van rocked violently under Jonas's feet. He toppled over the side and plummeted toward the alley floor.

Jonas screamed. The world spun in a blur before his eyes. He flailed his arms, reaching out for anything to stop his free fall. He felt the ladder rail brush his fingers and latched onto the frigid metal as tightly as he could. His fall was broken, but the momentum swung him into the side of the van. The impact flung CatBob out of the book bag.

The peachy feline yowled. He twisted his body in the air and managed to snag the bottom of Jonas's feathered top with his claws. There he hung, swinging wildly from side to side as Jonas attempted to regain his footing. CatBob looked down and saw the Beast's jaws rushing toward him. He lifted his legs out of the monster's jaws just before they slammed shut.

"We lost CatBob!" Neil cried.

"I'm still here," CatBob called back. "Just climb, Jonas—quickly!"

Jonas grabbed the next rung and pulled. He couldn't move. He glanced down and saw one of his chicken feet was trapped in the Beast's frothing jaws.

"It's got me!" he shrieked. "I can't move!"

CatBob hooked his front claws into the bottom hem of Jonas's costume and lowered himself down.

"Let go of that chicken foot!" he hissed.

He kicked at the Beast's snout. Razor-sharp claws dug into the monster's flesh and it released Jonas's foot, but only for a second.

"Climb!" CatBob yelled as he clambered up the feathers and back into the bag.

Jonas reached the roof and peered over the side. The Beast circled the van like a shark, baring its fangs and barking promises of terror. Jonas slid down the windshield and leapt off the hood.

He crashed to ground, tumbling awkwardly to avoid smashing the book bag and came to rest face down in a carpet of lush grass.

"I think we made it, guys!" he moaned.

CatBob and Neil spilled out of the bag and looked around. They were in a back yard secured on all sides by a tall, sturdy, wooden privacy fence. They heard the Beast on the other side, whining, sniffing, and frantically scratching at the planks. But after a few moments, the headlights from an approaching car sent the creature retreating into the night.

The three friends were safe for now, but they knew the Beast would be back soon enough.

12
THE DUSENBURY WEREWOLF

Jonas woke up stiff and sore the next morning. He had to hobble around for a while before he was able to walk normally, but the pain was worth it. Although the Beast had given him and his friends a scare, it didn't *get* any of the cats on East Newcomb Road.

He staggered out of the kitchen and crossed the yard to the garage, where he stood before the map, staring at the red circle.

What exactly is going on in the Dusenbury House? Jonas wondered. *Blackjack said the Beast had emerged from the hedges and chased Tiger, but what was it doing there? Was it following the same scent of chicken, or does it live there as a pet? Or maybe...*

Jonas ran back into the house and logged on to his computer. He typed "wolf" into a search engine and began clicking through the screenful of images it retrieved. They looked like the Beast, or at least what he could remember.

Maybe the Beast was an exotic pet that belonged to the owner of the Dusenbury House—if, in fact, a *person* actually lived there. But if so, why would they allow something so big to run free through the neighborhood?

That didn't seem likely to Jonas because the police would've have been called in to deal with the owner by now. Jonas had heard about that type of thing before at his mom's office.

The only other explanation he could think of was that the wolf *was* the owner of the Dusenbury House. He added "were" to his search word.

Jonas scrolled through illustrations and stills from werewolf movies, but they didn't look anything like the animal he'd encountered. The Beast didn't walk on its hind legs, it didn't have big muscles, and it wasn't wearing human clothes. He clicked on a web encyclopedia entry for "werewolf."

The web site defined a werewolf as "a mythological or folkloric human with the ability to shapeshift into a wolf or a therianthropic hybrid wolf-like creature, either purposefully or after being placed under a curse or affliction."

Jonas didn't know what *therianthropic* meant, but the rest stoked his suspicion that the thing he saw in the window of the Dusenbury House was the were-wolf in human form. The creature that had chased him looked skinny and the face he'd seen in the window earlier that night was skeletal.

Maybe the werewolf is being forced out of its house to hunt because it's starving to death, Jonas thought.

Or maybe not. There were too many questions to answer before he could consider such a theory. Like, why was the werewolf going after cats, and *only* cats? The encyclopedia page made no mention of were-wolves eating cats—or anything else for that matter.

Jonas's research was interrupted when he heard his dad's voice behind him.

"I have some time today, so I can take the costume back to the antique mall," he said from the doorway. "Where is it?"

Jonas sank down in his chair. "I don't know. I thought it was in the laundry," he answered, calmly stuffing white feathers down his shirt collar.

"Okay. Well, if you find it, let me know," Mr. Shurmann called as he disappeared down the hall.

Jonas logged off the computer and went up to his room.

He was greeted by two pairs of small, furry legs dangling off the edge of his bed; one gray and one peach-colored.

"What are you guys doing here?" he whispered.

CatBob and Neil lay on their backs, legs splayed, relaxed and content.

"We were waiting for you, but we got lonely and your bed is so soft and smells like you," CatBob said sleepily, "so we decided to lie down for a bit. And then, well, we got really comfortable. So..." his voice dissolved into a big yawn.

"We were concerned," Neil added. "We wanted to make sure you were okay, *and* we wanted to thank you for saving our hides. That was a very brave thing you did, Jonas."

"I was scared, that's all," Jonas said. "I've never seen a wolf up close, and I don't think I ever want to see another one."

"You're sure it was a wolf?" CatBob asked.

"Well, no. I saw..." Jonas stammered, "...I saw a skeletal face in a window of the Dusenbury House last night." He sank to his knees.

"Who was it?" CatBob asked.

"'Or *what* was it?'" Jonas muttered. "I didn't want to believe it was really a ghost, but it didn't look like it was living." His voice was shaky and his face looked drawn. "And then when I saw the Beast... Well, I just looked up wolves on the Internet, and the Beast looks kind of the same. But that's not even the worst part."

CatBob and Neil walked to the edge of the bed. They listened to their friend with wide eyes and swishing tails.

"It's just a theory, but..." Jonas took a deep breath, "...what if the skeletal face I saw in the window isn't a ghost, but a living person that's changing into a wolf—into the Beast, I mean—at night?"

"A human that can change into a wolf?" Neil exclaimed. "Is that even possible? Is that a real thing?"

"It's called a werewolf," Jonas said. "I don't think there's any evidence that werewolves really exist, but..." Jonas's thoughts trailed off.

Neil became rigid with alarm. "Jeezy Pete! I certainly hope there's no such thing as one of these 'werewolves,'" he said, "because if there is, it could most certainly *get* us—all of us! It's a human when it pets you, and then it turns into the Beast and— *MEOW!*—it *gets* you." He thwacked his tail on the bed furiously. "You can't even see it coming."

"Calm down, Neil," CatBob said. "It's only a theory, and not a very likely one at that. But Jonas is right to bring it up. We're detectives, so it's our duty to consider any and all possibilities, right?"

Neil nodded. "I suppose so."

"Okay, guys," Jonas said, "I have to get ready for work at the Pinchy Cage, so I have to change.

If there's anything else you want to tell me before I take this off, do it now." Jonas had wrestled off his shirt and was preparing to peel off his sweaty feathers.

CatBob piped up, "I don't think the Beast could be one of these werewolves you described, because it doesn't smell human. It doesn't exactly smell like a dog either, but definitely *not* human."

Jonas smiled. "See, Neil, nothing to worry about. Werewolves don't exist—at least not in Ohio—so you're safe."

Jonas tossed his costume on the floor and began digging through his dresser in search of a clean shirt. He turned back around to find his partners rubbing their drooling faces in the stinky feathers.

He scooped up the duo and smuggled them out the back door, then headed to the laundry room. But before he could toss the costume into the washer, Mr. Shurmann appeared in the doorway.

"Oh! You found it," he said. "Good. I'll take it back while you're helping your mom."

Jonas panicked. His life had changed so much since getting the costume, he couldn't imagine living without it. He wouldn't be able to talk to his best friends or help them find the missing cats. And they would have to face the Beast alone.

His palms began to sweat. He felt sick. Jonas was petrified, unable to move a muscle, but somehow his brain was working normally—actually faster than normal.

"I— I need it," he blurted.

"Oh?" his dad returned, "What for?"

"I got invited to a late costume party," Jonas said coolly, "and the only costumes that'll be left in the stores are the ones no one wants anyway."

Jonas was shocked how easily he rattled off this lie. He had no idea where it had come from. He felt like he was the third person in the room, listening to himself—and believing every word!

"So I might as well be the Chicken-Boy again," he added. "Everyone's already used to the costume."

Mr. Shurmann shrugged. "Okay. I'll put it in your room when it's clean. Have a good time at work," he called, "and mind your mother."

Jonas turned on the washer and took off for the veterinary office.

He heaved a sigh of relief when he got outside. He had no idea how he'd concocted the story he told his dad. He felt horrible for lying, but there was no way he could afford to lose the power of the costume right now. And there was no way in the world he was going to try to explain the *real* reason he wanted to keep it.

It was a tough spot Jonas found himself in. A part of him felt like he was living a lie: sneaking out after curfew, running the streets after dangerous animals, and lying to his father. But he knew without him and the costume, his friends wouldn't be able to find the missing cats and return them to their families. And it was obvious that no one else was going to do it. Jonas felt like he had no choice. There were too many people—and cat-friends—counting on him to give up now.

13

RESCUE!

Jonas sat on a swing alone during recess. He was trying to figure out how he and his partners could track the Beast back to its owner—if indeed one existed—when he felt his swing jolt to a sudden stop.

He looked up. Danny Martin stood looming over him, wearing a mischievous grin.

"Whatcha doin'?" said Danny.

"Nothing," Jonas mumbled, "just thinking about stuff."

"Good." Danny grabbed Jonas and pulled him away from the swing set. "We need one more to even out the teams."

"Where are we going?" Jonas asked.

"We're gonna play two-hand touch," Danny sneered, "or are you afraid of getting tagged,

Chicken-Boy?"

They marched into the open schoolyard where a group of boys had gathered.

"See," Danny shouted, "I told you the Chicken-Boy would play."

"All right, let's pick teams!" the tallest boy commanded. Jonas recognized him as Isaac Trent.

Isaac was two years older than Jonas and Danny and more athletic than any kid in school. Everyone said he was going to be a star football player when he got to junior high. This made Isaac popular like Danny, but unlike Danny, he didn't pick on other kids. At least, Jonas had never noticed it if he did. Isaac had always been nice to Jonas.

Regardless, Jonas disliked playing football. And waiting to be picked for teams was the part he disliked the most, because he'd never actually been chosen for a team his whole life. Jonas was *always* the last kid left; the kid no one wanted on their team.

Jonas just wasn't cut out for football. He was skinny, which made him a good runner, but he lacked the muscles to throw a ball, tackle, or take a hit.

Danny and Isaac voted themselves captains and began selecting players. Soon, the pool dwindled to Jonas and Billy Keitzer; a boy only slightly more athletic than Jonas. Danny chose Billy, which meant Jonas was on Isaac's team—like always, by default.

"Come on, Jonas, huddle up!" Isaac called.

Jonas shuffled to his team and the game was underway.

The players had taken their positions awaiting the snap, when Jonas heard someone chanting, "Bock-bock chicken!" A brief ripple of laughter passed through the line then Isaac shouted, "Hike!"

Everyone sprang into a chaotic fray of running and shoving, but Jonas never even made it as far as the running part. He'd been placed opposite a boy who was much bigger than he, and as soon as the snap was made, the larger boy bulldozed Jonas to the ground. Isaac pulled Jonas to his feet after the play ended.

"Sorry, Isaac," Jonas said, "I'm just not very good at football."

"Nah, it's my fault for putting you on defense," Isaac said. "How 'bout we have you run next time?"

For the next play, Isaac designated Jonas as a receiver. He explained to Jonas that all he had to do was run as far past the other team as he could while keeping his eye on Isaac and the ball. And if Isaac threw the ball to him, then his job was to catch it and run all the way to the fence. Jonas didn't really understand football, but this was a concept even *he* could grasp.

The ball was snapped and Jonas took off. Danny

Martin and another kid tried to cover him, but struggled to keep up. Jonas widened the gap and glanced back just in time to see Isaac launch the ball into the blue sky.

He panicked.

Jonas couldn't keep his eyes on Danny *and* his friend *and* the ball all at once, so he chose one.

He hooked left and the pigskin slammed into his chest with a painful *smack*. Jonas hugged the ball to his body and ran as fast as he could. When he reached the fence, a commotion erupted behind him. Jonas turned to see Isaac and the rest of the team cheering—for him!

His mouth contorted into an insuppressible grin as his teammates showered him with backslaps and attaboys. For the first time in his life, Jonas felt accepted by his classmates, which felt strange— even stranger than talking to cats.

The players resumed their positions at the line of scrimmage and waited for the next snap, but it never came.

Instead of the usual, "Hut! Hut! Hike!" Danny called out, "Bock-bock chicken!" which was met with uproarious laughter. But the laughter was cut short by a shrill scream and the sound of screeching tires.

Jonas stood up and spied a group of girls gathered at the fence across the schoolyard watching a car that had suddenly stopped. The driver leaped out and began running around in the street.

As the boys drew closer, they saw a gray cat running a zig-zag path through the road. Another car slammed on its brakes just in time to avoid the berserk feline. When the cat ran onto the sidewalk, Jonas saw the reason for its odd behavior; its head was caught in a dirty plastic sandwich bag. The cat was running blind.

"Sweet," Jonas heard Danny say to his friends, "that stupid cat's gonna get flattened by a car."

More kids crowded the fence, watching as the panicked feline barely escaped the wheels of a third car. Teachers blew their whistles and waded through the mob to see what was happening.

Jonas tapped Isaac on the shoulder and whispered in his ear. The older boy nodded and took off across the schoolyard with Jonas following close behind.

Jonas directed Isaac to a spot just ahead of the cat's path. When Isaac reached the tall fence, he kneeled down with his hands cupped in front of him. Jonas planted a foot in Isaac's palms and was launched up and over the fence with a loud, "Alley-oop!" Jonas dropped to the ground on the opposite side and tumbled to his feet.

Kids swarmed the fence, cheering as he ran toward the panicked feline.

He discovered the cat wasn't completely blind when it nimbly dodged his grasp and continued trotting down the road. Jonas chased after the fuzzy runaway in the awkward, bent waddle that people instinctively adopt when chasing small animals.

"It's okay," he called. "You can stop running. I just want to get the bag off your head."

But his words made no difference; the cat trotted on, seemingly unaware of him.

A black car swung around the corner just ahead of the pair. The squeal of the tires startling the feline out of the street and into a nearby alley, but Jonas was frozen in his tracks.

When Jonas spotted the oncoming car, his first thought was to follow the cat. But then he considered running in the opposite direction. Then panic set in and his mind began to race. His head overloaded with so many thoughts that he couldn't make sense of any of them. And since his brain couldn't make a decision, it couldn't tell his body what to do. So Jonas just stood still as the car barreled toward him.

He kept expecting the car to come to a sudden, screeching stop, but it didn't. A moment later, the bumper was too close for Jonas to run out of its way. That's when his head cleared and only one thought remained: *jump!*

Jonas held his breath and leaped as high as he

could. His sneakers landed on the hood with a loud *thud!* He scampered up the windshield, rolled over the roof, slid down the rear windshield, and sprang off of the trunk. His feet touched the pavement just as the car finally jerked to a stop.

The driver-side door flew open. A bald, fat man rocked side to side, bellowing curses as he struggled to free himself from the seat belt.

"Are you crazy, kid?!" he roared. "You almost gave me a heart attack! Just you wait till I get out of here."

The children behind the fence giggled but Jonas had no interest in waiting for the man to get free. Jonas turned and bolted into the alley just in time to see a gray tail slip around a garage. He followed after it and found the cat huddled on the back stoop of a house.

Jonas slowly kneeled and spoke in a soothing tone. "Hey, little guy, I'm a friend," he cooed. "I just want to get that bag off your head so you can see again."

The trembling feline responded with a stream of strained cries. Jonas inched closer. He managed to pinch the corner of the bag between his thumb and forefinger, but the motion spooked the cat and it bolted, wrenching the plastic from his grasp.

Jonas chased the runaway around the house and down the sidewalk, while gasping promises of his good intentions. But the feline ran on regardless of what he said.

That's when Jonas realized he wasn't wearing his chicken costume, which meant he couldn't talk to this cat like he did to CatBob and Neil. To this little guy, Jonas sounded like any other human, and worse, the cat's hearing was probably impaired by the bag.

The pair ran across the street, down the opposite sidewalk, then around another house. There, Jonas managed to corral the frightened feline into a corner of the yard that was edged by a weathered picket fence. He moved in swiftly, and this time, managed to snatch the bag off of the cat's head before it pulled away.

The cat crouched down and looked up at Jonas. The stream of distressed cries began to abate. Jonas backed up and offered his hand to the cat to smell.

It stepped forward and sniffed him, then sauntered through the gate into the alley where it squatted and took a runny poop on the asphalt.

"I guess that would have scared the crap out of me too," Jonas said to his new friend. "But you can relax now, you're okay."

The cat returned with friendly meows and tail hugs. It looked up at him through a pair of brilliant, but crossed, blue eyes. Jonas noticed its coat was clean to the touch and had the distinct markings of a Siamese with the addition of stripes, which Jonas knew purebred Siamese cats didn't have.

"You're too clean to be a stray," he said, "so you obviously have a home. But how are we going to find your family if you don't have tags?"

The cat rubbed its face against Jonas's sneaker and purred.

"There you are! You scared me to death. What are you—" Jonas turned to see one of the teachers from his school, Mrs. Mason, standing at the gate. She fell silent when she saw the cat.

"This was stuck on his head." Jonas held up the scummy freezer bag. "He was blinded and almost got run over, but I managed to get it off of him before he was hurt."

"And I see he's thankful that you did." Mrs. Mason said, watching the cat rub against Jonas's leg. "Jonas Shurmann—don't ever run into the street like that again!" she scolded.

"I'm sorry. I just had to do something. When I first saw him running, I heard some kids say it was funny that he would get run over," Jonas looked down at the cat and frowned. "No one was going to do anything. He needed my help."

"Yes, well, don't ever do it again. If something like this happens, you're to tell me or another teacher—no running into the street," she huffed.

"What are we going to do with him?" Jonas asked. "I don't know where he lives. He isn't wearing tags."

"You'll have to bring him back to the school, I suppose," she said. "We'll figure out the rest later."

Mrs. Mason walked Jonas and his new friend back to the school where his classmates were still gathered at the fence. A cheer went up from the crowd as Jonas rounded the corner with the cat in his arms.

Jonas was confused by the applause and looked around to see what the cheering was for. "What's going on?" he asked. "Why are they cheering?"

Mrs. Mason looked down at Jonas and smiled. "For you, of course," she chuckled. "For saving this poor cat's life. You're a hero!"

14

THE CHICKEN-BOY OF CLINTONVILLE

Despite stiff muscles from two days of running—both from the Beast, and after the cat with a freezer bag stuck on its head—Jonas ran all the way home after school.

He burst through the door and searched the house for his dad, eventually discovering him in the kitchen. Jonas was still winded from the run home, but was much too excited about his news to wait long enough to catch his breath. Instead, he frantically panted out the events of the day to his bewildered father.

He told his dad how Danny Martin had forced him to play football, which led to Jonas scoring his very first touchdown. He told him about the cat with a bag on its head, and explained how Isaac boosted him over the fence. He gave the blow-by-blow of the chase through the neighborhood that ended in Jonas managing to remove the bag, saving the cat from death. And the best part: when Jonas and Mrs. Mason got back to school, how all of Jonas's classmates cheered for him. Jonas said he did all of that without the...

Jonas stopped.

Mr. Shurmann's eyebrows were raised in anticipation of the conclusion. "Without *what*, Jonas?" he asked.

"Where's my chicken costume?"

Mr. Shurmann suddenly looked guilty. "I, uh, I'm taking it back to the antique mall today. I was just about to leave, actually," he muttered. "I know you said you'd wear it to the party, but I also know the kids in your class made fun of it, and I don't want you to go through that to save my feelings. I was trying to surprise you, but I just didn't think it through." Mr. Shurmann looked at the floor. "I remember being your age and I know standing out for the wrong reasons isn't what you want, so I'm going to get you another—"

"I don't want another costume," Jonas said firmly, "I want the one you gave me." He hadn't meant to cut his father off, it just came out. "At first I thought it looked ridiculous too, but I've made the best friends I've ever had because I wore that costume, and I don't give a rat's butt if Danny Martin, or anyone else, thinks it looks dorky. I think it's the coolest costume ever, and I'm grateful you got it for me instead of something everyone else has."

Mr. Shurmann cleared his throat and pushed his glasses up. "Well," he chuckled, "how can I argue with that?"

A couple hours later, Jonas was back in his costume, performing a house-to-house canvassing with his feline partners.

Jonas had filled his book bag with a new flier that featured a complete list of the missing cats along with descriptions and "last seen" addresses. The contact information for Shurmann Veterinary Hospital was printed at the top.

Jonas explained to the residents how cats often get trapped in garages and sheds while exploring. He asked everyone with a garage or shed to check them that evening and call the hospital if they found any cats.

A few people teased Jonas that he was late for Halloween, but most complimented him on both his costume and his cute cat-friends. Jonas just smiled and thanked them before moving on to the next house.

Lugging the huge stack of fliers all over the neighborhood was tough work, but Jonas didn't complain.

He and his friends were determined to find the missing cats, no matter what it took.

And unbeknownst to the detectives, a few of the people they spoke to couldn't resist snapping some pictures of them as they marched down the sidewalk. One of the photos was uploaded to *The Clintonville Social Network*.

The caption under the image read, CLINTONVILLE CHICKEN-BOY AND HIS FURRY FRIENDS. Within an hour, it had become the most reposted image on the site. A few users posted that their child went to George Clinton Elementary with the Chicken-Boy and that he'd saved a cat at school that very day. The detectives were an instant sensation.

The residents all agreed the Chicken-Boy was the official neighborhood superhero.

15
MY HERO

After Jonas dropped off CatBob and Neil at their homes, he shuffled on toward his own. He couldn't wait to eat. The savory aromas of fresh-cooked meals wafted from every house he passed, drawing growls from his empty stomach.

He stumbled through the door to find his mom waiting for him at the kitchen table with a plate of leftovers. He sat down without a word and began to eat.

Jonas couldn't remember when food tasted so good. He usually didn't care for meatloaf, but he found himself savoring every delicious bite after a long day at school and an evening spent walking all over the neighborhood.

"Where have you been?" his mother finally asked.

Jonas produced a flier from his book bag and slid it across the table. "We were looking for the missing cats," he said.

"Did you have any luck finding them?"

"No." Jonas frowned at his plate.

"Well, you did a good thing by informing people," his mother said. "Fewer cats will probably go missing because of your fliers." She paused and then cleared her throat and said, "In fact, one of the teachers at your school, Mrs. Mason, brought a cat in this afternoon. She told me you had quite a day at school."

"Uh-oh," Jonas breathed.

"What happened?"

"I made my first touchdown today..." Jonas sighed. "...and I chased a cat that had a freezer bag stuck on its head. I know I shouldn't have done it," he added, "Mrs. Mason already told me." He looked up at his mother with wide eyes. "You should have seen him, Mom. He was just so happy to be able to breathe again. He almost died because someone didn't cut the bag before they threw it in the trash."

Mrs. Shurmann propped her head in her hands. "That happens a lot," she said. "That cat was very lucky that you cared enough to save him."

"I told him that I would be his friend from now on," Jonas said. "And not just him, but every cat."

"I thought 'cats had it easy,'" his mother said.

Jonas hadn't told anyone how he'd felt about cats except for Neil, and that was before he found out Neil could understand him. His mom must have heard him talking to himself at work. Hearing her say it out loud made him realize how ignorant he'd been. Jonas felt ashamed of himself. His face was flushed from embarrassment.

"My new friends taught me that that isn't true," he said. "When Mrs. Mason walked me back to school with the cat, everyone was cheering because I saved it—even Danny Martin and his friends. They said I was a hero." Jonas pushed scraps with his fork. "I thought that's what I've always wanted people to think of me, but it didn't feel as good as making that touchdown. It felt like I didn't really deserve those cheers, like I..." Jonas paused, searching for the right words. "I'd already gotten what I wanted. I wanted the bag off of the cat's head so it wouldn't die." Jonas fell silent for a while and then asked, "Am I grounded?"

Mrs. Shurmann's eyes welled up with tears. "No," she said. "How could I possibly deprive Clintonville of its famous Chicken-Boy?" She hugged Jonas and kissed his head, then whispered, "Don't *ever* run out into the street again. You're smarter than that."

16
GHOST
TOWN

The next afternoon, Jonas rode his bike through the neighborhood with CatBob and Neil hitching along in his book bag. The felines had protested at first, but Jonas explained that for them to get everywhere they needed to go, it was either the bike or a car. The cats chose the bike.

"So, why is it that dogs like car rides and cats don't?" Jonas asked his friends.

"Well, cats always have to be in control of their surroundings," Neil said, "or at the very least, we have to be aware of them. That's why we investigate everything. And since we cats can't control cars, we feel vulnerable in them, unsafe."

"I think I understand," Jonas said. "So, why do dogs like car rides so much?"

"Who knows," Neil said. "Why do dogs look at

a litter box and see dinner?"

"Eww, gross!" Jonas laughed.

The trio spent the afternoon and early evening wheeling through the neighborhood, advising every cat they encountered to stay indoors until the Beast had been captured. They were met with suspicion and even some hisses, but Neil explained that those reactions were to be expected.

"It's just a cat's nature to be wary of anything new or different," Neil said.

But despite the fuss, the felines seemed to take the warning to heart. Shortly after the detectives delivered the message, the cats announced that they would rather be inside; not because they were told to, but because they *wanted* to go in.

That's just how it worked with cats, Neil explained—everything had to be *their* idea.

The trio turned homeward as night fell. CatBob and Neil scanned every yard, every alleyway, and every bush they passed on the way. As far as they could see, their mission had been a success. The streets were completely absent of any feline presence.

Jonas dropped his friends at their homes, then decided to take one last spin through the neighborhood.

He rode past the Clintonville Community

Market, where his family shopped. Tall corn shocks flanked the entrance and a pyramid of pumpkins occupied the seating area. Members of a scooter club were gathered out front. They waved and cheered as Jonas rolled by. He smiled and waved back as he pedaled on toward East North Dusenbury Street.

When Jonas stopped to check out the Halloween Tree in the daylight, he realized he'd mostly ignored the yard displays this season. That was a shame, since Halloween was Jonas's favorite time of year. So, he decided to take a look around before everything was packed away for winter. Fortunately, Jonas's neighbors loved Halloween as much as he did and were in no hurry to remove the Styrofoam gravestones and plastic skeletons from their yards. However, shortly into the tour, the scenery changed from store bought set pieces to the only real life Halloween display in the neighborhood: the Dusenbury House.

It loomed like a giant brick skull, gazing into a secret world only the dead could see. But Jonas suspected the mansion only *appeared* dead and vacant to lull the neighborhood into a false sense of security. And as soon as people let their guard down, he was sure the house would burst through the hedgerow and wreak havoc upon all of Clintonville.

Danny Martin might be right about me having too much candy, he thought. *Maybe it really is just a creepy* old house and maybe I really am letting my imagination runaway. After all, there are no such things as ghosts or werewolves, right?

He was turning to leave when he noticed something move in a third-floor window.

"Oh, no!" he gasped.

Jonas gripped his handlebars and hoped with all his might that it was *just* his imagination. But he had to be sure, so he retrieved a set of binoculars from his book bag.

The lenses revealed the tattered red curtain was swaying as if it had been moved a moment before. He adjusted the focus. As the edges of the world became sharp again, the curtain was suddenly yanked aside. The gulf of darkness beyond betrayed no movement, no shape, nor any sign of life.

Jonas held his breath, anticipating something terrible, but nothing happened.

He lowered the binoculars and looked around, hoping to see someone he knew walking or riding their bike, but the sidewalks were deserted.

He brought the lenses back to his face just in time to see a pair of eyes blink open in the void.

They looked right at him.

Jonas screamed. He threw the binoculars in his bag and pedaled home as fast as he could.

17
THE
BEAST
STRIKES!

The detectives gathered in the garage the next afternoon, prepping for another round of canvassing. Jonas packed another stack of "missing" fliers while the cats plotted their route on the map. CatBob told Jonas to prepare to get wet; the broken end of his tail was aching and that always meant rain was nearby. Jonas donned his raincoat and the friends were on their way.

The detectives found people more receptive to their message this time. Many residents claimed they'd seen the trio on *The Clintonville Social Network* and asked for a picture with them. Jonas agreed as long as they promised to take a flier and listen to his speech about the dangers of garages. Afterward, the friends thanked the residents and marched to the next house to do it all over again.

The day was unusually warm and muggy for autumn. The heat had Jonas sweating under his feathers and raincoat, making the stiff winds that blew in at sunset a welcome relief.

"We'd better head back," CatBob said, nodding at the glowing street lamps. "My tail's killing me!"

"I guess so. Especially since you two don't have raincoats," Jonas answered.

They turned back and saw dark shelf clouds looming on the horizon. The ragged undersides looked as if they might scrape the rooftops of the taller houses. A sudden gale whipped the trees into motion. Gnarled branches waved a warning that time was running out.

"Looks like it's really going to come down," Jonas called. "Sorry guys, I didn't know the storm would be this bad."

The trio quickened their pace but Jonas was struggling under the weight of the fliers.

Swarms of leaves rose from the street and churned around the trio. A distant peal of thunder heralded the arrival of the storm.

Big, fat raindrops splattered noisily on the pavement. They were so heavy that Jonas initially thought someone was pelting his raincoat with rocks. The cats' skin jumped from the shock of the frigid water.

Jonas could see the intersection of East North Dusenbury and Moors Avenue ahead. It was completely deserted. Apparently the detectives were the only ones that had failed to anticipate the bad weather.

"Wait up, guys!" Jonas panted as he clutched his side. "This bag is super heavy. Just give me a second to catch my breath."

The felines trotted back, then paused. Their ears perked as an eerie silence fell over the street and a howl rose briefly in the stillness. Jonas's pulse quickened and the hackles rose on CatBob's and Neil's backs.

"We need to go—now!" CatBob said, scanning the street.

By the time Jonas had managed to hobble to the intersection, he found himself alone. He turned around and saw his partners watching the mouth of the alley they'd just passed where a familiar figure was staggering from the shadows.

CatBob flattened his ears and trotted toward the Beast. Jonas called after him but a clap of thunder drowned his voice. He slipped his book bag off and replaced the stack of fliers with Neil.

When he rose he found CatBob and the Beast facing off. Jonas approached carefully. He wanted to grab CatBob, but was afraid the Beast would attack if he did. Instead he tried calling out again, but this time a sudden powerful gust took his breath away. Tall trees bent backward and a Jonas was blinded by a flurry of leaves. Then the rain came roaring down from the sky.

Jonas stumbled blindly ahead, watching the two figures crouched in the deluge. Lightning flashed. CatBob bolted with the Beast right on his heels.

Jonas followed them around the corner as the pair raced up Dusenbury Street. The Beast overtook CatBob just as the feline-detective reached the wild hedgerow. The brute cut him off, forcing CatBob through the opening.

Jonas screamed as the monster charged in after.

He dove headfirst through the opening, into thorny branches that scratched his face and tugged the hood of his raincoat back. He emerged on the other side half-blind from the rain. He squinted against the water and found his peachy partner with his back arched, poised to strike. Jonas reached out to grab his friend, but drew his hand back when the feline growled. CatBob was staring straight through Jonas—at something behind him. Jonas sat up and turned around.

Two amber eyes cast a burning glare through the cold rain. Jonas was so close to the Beast he could smell the rot on its breath.

18
THE DUSENBURY HOUSE

The Beast's growl rattled Jonas's rib cage. His heart fluttered and he suddenly felt dizzy. Jonas barely caught himself as he fell backward into the tall grass. As he did, his fingers brushed something hidden among the long blades. The Beast opened its jaws and lunged. Jonas squeezed his eyes shut, lifted the object out of the grass, and swung it as hard as he could.

The object connected with an audible *thud!* Jonas braced himself for the pain of the brute's teeth, but it never came. He opened his eyes in time to see the monster disappear around the side of the house. He dropped the tree branch and turned back to CatBob, who was still poised to attack. Jonas dumped the skinny feline into his book bag and hugged it to his chest to shield his partners from the rainstorm.

Thunder shook the muddy ground under his knees as howling gales drove the rain in sheets. The bare and broken trees overhead offered no shelter and the porch stood exposed to the lashing rain. Jonas didn't know how much more he could endure. He considered making a run for the school or home, but he knew the Beast was still close by, watching. It would definitely try to get him and his partners again as soon as it had recovered from the blow he'd dealt it. That's when Jonas heard a creaking sound creep through the din of the rain and into his ear.

He looked up to find the front door of the Dusenbury House had swung open. A faint blue light flickered from within, beckoning him to enter.

Jonas hesitated. He heard snarling coming from the side of the house.

It's probably more dangerous to stay out here with Beast then to face whatever's in the house, he thought.

Lightning split the sky. The earth rattled under the awesome thunderclap that followed.

Jonas leapt to his feet. "Hang on, guys!" he shouted. He gripped the bag and charged into the jaws of the brick monster that had occupied his imagination for days.

He slammed the door behind him and sank to his knees. The house was completely dark. Jonas glanced around the gloom, holding the bag, trying to figure out if they were alone. After a few tense moments a series of lightning flashes illuminated the front hall. As far as he could tell, they were safe, at least for the moment.

He placed the sopping book bag on the floor and gently unzipped it. "Come on out, guys, but stay close to me," he whispered. "I didn't think we'd last out there with the Beast hunting us. The front door opened, and, well, I had no choice."

The two felines tumbled out together.

"We're inside the Dusenbury House?" CatBob asked as he shook off the wet.

"We sure are," Jonas whispered. He removed his flashlight and switched it on. The bluish beam revealed walls of crumbling plaster and peeling wallpaper.

Neil's tail made s curves as he sniffed the worn floorboards and tattered rugs. "Anything has to be better than being tossed around in that bag," he said as he tapped the rug with his paw and waited for a reaction.

"Sorry," Jonas said, "but I didn't want CatBob to end up missing like the other cats that ran through those bushes."

"You didn't have to do that, you know," CatBob put in. "I could have handled that mangy cur myself.

He wasn't so tough."

Jonas smirked. "Yeah? Well, he scared me plenty."

"Well, I guess he was kind of scary," CatBob admitted. "Thanks, Jonas," he muttered.

"That was very gentlemanly of you, CatBob," Neil cooed. He rubbed his cheek against his friend. "I'm very proud of you!"

"Yeah, yeah, keep it to yourself," CatBob said. "Let's not forget Jonas saw a werewolf in this house."

"Shhh!" Neil hissed. The plump gray cat stood erect, ears pricked, listening intently. "Do you hear that? How odd."

Jonas and CatBob listened. CatBob heard it too.

"Yes. What is that?" the peach feline whispered.

Jonas strained his ears and held his breath but all he could hear was the throbbing of his pulse and the muffled din of the storm outside. He crouched beside his companions. That's when he heard a strange noise coming from the end of the hall, where the blue light flickered.

Jonas thought it sounded like a voice, but it never stopped. It was the sound of constant talking, but the owner of the voice wasn't human.

"It sounds like a robot," Jonas whispered.

The cats looked at him, puzzled.

"A robot?" Neil asked. "What sort of robot? Is it a robot that could *get* me?"

"I don't know, maybe. I'm not sure that's what it is. I mean, if there *is* a werewolf in here, I don't know why he would need a robot." Jonas started down the hall. "Come on. Whatever it is, we're going to find out."

The trio passed under a series of ornate picture frames. The unfriendly faces in the photos glared down at the detectives, as if to warn them their presence in the house was known—and unwelcome.

Then the friends came to a doorway. The flashlight beam illuminated towers of cardboard boxes stacked against the walls labeled "books." A desk squatted under a dune of loose papers and hardback volumes in the center of the room. The rest of the furniture sat abandoned under white sheets. The room looked as though it hadn't been visited in years.

A little farther down the hall the detectives discovered a dining room, or at least that's what it used to be. The long dining table was presently occupied by an enormous pile of toys: Frisbees, baseballs, footballs, kites, a remote control helicopter, a couple of model rockets, a Styrofoam glider, Wiffle Balls, maroon kick balls like the ones used in Jonas's gym class, and even some books—schoolbooks!

Jonas rifled through the pile, but his math book

wasn't among them.

"Sorry, guys," Jonas whispered, "I thought one of these books might have been..."

A clap of thunder rattled the floorboards under his feet. The house's wooden skeleton groaned under the fury of the raging wind. Jonas looked down to check on his friends only to discover he was alone.

"Neil?" he called. "CatBob? Where'd you go, guys?"

Jonas shone the beam down the hall, but there was no sign of them. He took a deep breath. Even though he was scared, running away and deserting his friends in the Dusenbury House was not an option. And unlike Neil, Jonas was a human boy who knew there were no such thing as werewolves—especially ones with killer robots. At least he hoped... He *really* hoped. Because even if there were such things, he was going to have to find his friends—werewolves with killer robots or not.

Jonas padded down the hall toward the blue flickering light. The closer he got, the louder the robot voice grew. When he reached the end of the hall he found himself standing in the doorway to...a kitchen.

Jonas shone the light around to make sure he was alone, then switched it off. As soon as the beam died, he saw the source of the mysterious blue glow he'd been following.

It was a dishwasher door; a shiny, new, metal dishwasher door that was reflecting a blue light that originated from a doorway on the opposite side of the kitchen.

Jonas padded across the kitchen where he found a flight of wooden steps leading down to a basement. He stood by the doorway, listening to the robot voice. It was much louder now, but he still couldn't decipher the words through the electronic fuzz. Jonas looked around again, hoping to catch sight of his friends, but he was still alone.

Well, there's no other way out of this, he thought. *Whatever's waiting at the bottom of those steps has my two best friends and I have to save them, no matter what it is.*

19
THE GHOST

Jonas lowered his foot onto the first tread. The old board creaked under his weight. He winced, expecting something dreadful to emerge from the blue glow and grab him, but the light below betrayed no movement. The mysterious voice droned on.

Jonas cautiously padded down the rest of the stairs. When he reached the bottom, he gasped at what lay before him.

Small cardboard boxes had been arranged in two rows with a cat nestled in each one. Jonas smiled. The felines looked like bread loaves that had risen in their pans and sprouted ears and whiskers. He clicked on his flashlight and examined each one.

Among the felines was a tabby with a dark, marbled coat, sporting a worn red collar. Jonas crouched beside the cat and gently stroked its head. He flipped its tags over and smiled.

"Hello, Puck!" he whispered. "Your family's gonna be so happy I found you."

"Hello, boy," Puck purred. "Keep the pets coming, but please, don't drip on me; I'm too warm."

"Oh, sorry." Jonas carefully stroked the tabby's back, being mindful of his dripping raincoat.

He continued scanning the rows with the flashlight until the beam came to rest on a familiar sight. Jonas almost screamed when he spotted CatBob. The peachy feline was rubbing his wet cheek against a small black cat.

"CatBob!" Jonas whispered. "Where's Neil?"

CatBob didn't answer. He was busy licking his inky companion's head.

Jonas tiptoed over and crouched beside them, being careful not to drip on either of them. The black cat rumbled greetings.

"This is Cinderella," CatBob said. "We found her! And she's been safe here in this house the whole time." He looked up at Jonas and meowed with relief. "I don't know how, but it looks like *all* of the missing cats are here."

The robotic voice stopped. Jonas looked around, but all he could make out in the darkened room was a large television screen in the corner that bathed everything in an eerie blue glow.

So that's what was reflected on the dishwasher door, thought Jonas. *But who's controlling the sound?*

"Who's there?" he called.

"Don't worry, you're safe here," a voice boomed from the shadows. "The storm should be over soon."

CatBob trotted past Jonas and vanished into the darkness.

"CatBob! Wait—" Jonas stammered, but the feline was lost from sight.

"You must be a good guy to have such loyal friends as CatBob and Neil Higgins," the voice continued.

Jonas was sweating under his costume and raincoat. "I guess so," he mumbled. "How do *you* know them?"

"Oh, I see them almost every night on my walks. They're two of my favorite cat-friends to visit. Such characters; always up to something," the man chuckled. "I found them wandering way down the street the other night. They were visiting another group of cats on my route who were apparently throwing a wild cat party."

"A friend," Jonas whispered, remembering who the cats had told him had interrupted their investigation and taken CatBob and Neil home.

It also occurred to him that his partners had never

told him their friend's name because Jonas had asked when he wasn't wearing his costume.

"Yes, I'm a friend to all the cats around here," the man declared. "That's why I have to keep them safe until that monster is caught."

"The Beast, you mean. He almost got CatBob outside," Jonas said.

"He might have, had it not been for the brave actions of Clintonville's famous Chicken-Boy," the man said. "But I'm afraid your fliers won't help recover the missing cats. As you can see, they're in my care, and must remain here until the streets are safe again."

Jonas leapt to his feet. "But they aren't yours to keep! Their families are worried sick—"

"Spare me the sermon." The man fired back. "I know it's wrong, but people too often underestimate the dangers these little guys face. Most were lured here unintentionally by the chicken bait in my varmint traps. Apparently the raccoons that live in my attic are too clever to be caught in the cages, but cats, ha!—I've caught every other one in the neighborhood," the man chuckled. "And a good thing I did catch them, because the rest were chased here by the Beast. But once Animal Control captures it, I'll be more than happy to return every one of my guests to their families."

"What *is* the Beast, anyway?" Jonas asked.

"*Canis latrans*: commonly known as a prairie wolf or coyote. They usually only venture into cities when their own habitat's been invaded by humans, or when they've been abandoned by their guardians after being kept as pets," the man said. "I don't think it's rabid or anything like that; it's just trying to survive in an alien environment, but Clintonville is *not* its home. Too many small, four-legged residents live here for that."

Jonas heard a thump on the floor and a moment later CatBob sauntered out of the shadows. The peachy feline rubbed against Jonas's leg and purred.

A large figure rose from the corner and extend an arm toward the television. The robot voice returned.

"The severe thunderstorm warning for... Franklin County... has been allowed to expire," the voice droned. "At... eight thirty PM... National Weather Service Doppler radar indicated the storm moving over Columbus had weakened below severe limits..."

Jonas recognized the voice. It played along with the constant weather radar loop on the television screen. Jonas's dad had turned to that channel last summer when a scary storm had prompted a tornado warning.

"The rain will let up soon, then you three can

go," the man said. "I called your mom's office and notified them of your whereabouts already."

The figure stepped out of the shadows. A tall, chubby man stood before Jonas wearing a wild afro. His long beard and mustache parted to reveal a brilliant, toothy grin. He held Jonas's math book in his hand.

"I believe *this* is yours," he said.

As Jonas took the book and thanked the stranger, a shadow passed over his face. He was reminded of being taunted by Danny Martin and his friends.

Sensing the painful memory, the man said, "I used to get bullied in school too."

"Really?" Jonas asked. "How did you stop it?"

"I became a ghost." The man laughed at Jonas's surprised expression. "I'm Orville Dusenbury, by the way," he said as he extended his hand. "Son of the late Dr. Winslow Dusenbury."

Jonas shook his hand and said "I'm—"

"You're Jonas Shurmann, aka the famous Chicken-Boy of Clintonville," Orville announced with a dramatic flourish. "I know who you are. Everyone in the neighborhood knows who *you* are. You're a super-hero. You saved a cat from being run over and suffocated yesterday at school, and today you saved CatBob from the Beast, and soon you'll be known as the only kid to have entered the Dusenbury House and survived. You're practically a legend on the *Clintonville Social Network*—see?"

Orville held out his smart phone. The screen was filled with an image of Jonas, Neil, and CatBob, walking down the sidewalk. Under the image were the words, THE CLINTONVILLE CHICKEN-BOY AND HIS CRIME CATS. He then motioned to his guests to head upstairs.

As the three entered the kitchen, Jonas said, "I guess that explains why everyone's been excited to see us and take our fliers, but how did everyone know about me saving the cat at school?"

Orville laughed. "You can't do anything without *someone* posting about it online these days."

As they strolled down the hall, Jonas paused and shifted his weight awkwardly. "Mr. Dusenbury, I thought you were a ghost," he confessed.

"That's okay. I feel like it sometimes. Plus, I did use my father's old medical skeleton to peek out at you when I noticed you spying on my house," he chuckled, "so you can hardly be blamed for thinking I'm a ghost."

"I only spied on the house because I thought the Beast might've been a werewolf that lived here," Jonas said.

Orville threw back his head and laughed from his belly. "Oh! man, I'll have to remember that one. So

I guess my old house freaks everyone out, huh? Well, I can't blame people for thinking that the house is haunted since I'm the one who started that rumor," he gasped and wiped tears from his eyes. "But now that I've heard your brilliant werewolf story, I wish I'd used that one instead."

As they began climbing a grand staircase Jonas noted more antique photos hanging on the wall. Orville's house seemed to be a time capsule from a century ago.

"Why would you want people to think you're a ghost or a werewolf?" Jonas asked.

"I guess I've had to get on by myself for so long that I never consider the need to be accepted by others," Orville said. "That, and most people expected me to be like my father."

He halted next to a portrait of a man Jonas assumed was Dr. Winslow Dusenbury. The portrait was in color, unlike most of the others, but still looked very old to Jonas. The man in the photo wore a stern expression.

"I loved the guy, but he was too stuffy," Orville said. "He was always so concerned with other people's opinions. I never understood that. Be who you *genuinely* are, I say." Orville looked at Jonas with a mischievous gleam in his eye. "That's why I came back to Clintonville to live. It's changed from when

I grew up here under my father's household, into my kind of place, you know? I mean, what other neighborhood is defended by its very own Chicken-Boy superhero?"

When they reached the top of the stairs, Orville ushered Jonas over to a set of double doors and gently pushed them open. "And what other neighborhood has cats that can read?" he asked.

Inside, Jonas saw an old-fashioned library that looked like one Sherlock Holmes would have. Bookshelves crowded with leather-bound tomes stretched to the ceiling. Neil Higgins sat perched atop a stately kneehole desk at the other end of the room, a large book spread before him. The cyclopean feline looked up at his visitors triumphantly and chirped.

"Neil says he has a plan," Jonas announced.

"Then count me in!" Orville replied.

20
DANGEROUS MISSION

The three detectives traipsed up East Newcomb Road to a large yellow house. Jonas knocked on the door and immediately regretted it. He realized he had no idea what to say to the person that answered. He and his partners needed to see Blackjack, but Jonas hadn't considered that he was the only human he knew of that could talk to cats. He certainly couldn't expect Blackjack's family to bring her to the door at the request of some strange kid wearing a chicken costume after Halloween—*especially* one who says he can talk to cats.

Jonas heard footsteps inside. Before his brain could form a plan, the door swung open. A woman smiled down at the three callers.

"Well, aren't you cute," she sang. "I saw your pictures on the Clintonville social site. What can I do for you?"

Jonas just stood silent, dumbfounded.

"What are you doing?" Neil whispered. "Say something, why don't you?"

"I, umm—" Jonas started.

The woman's smile widened. "Yes? Go ahead," she nodded encouragingly.

A stream of stammers and mumbled noises poured from Jonas's mouth.

Neil ears swiveled back. "Good gravy, Jonas!" he exclaimed. "If you can't do it, I will."

The gray cat confidently toddled up to the woman's feet and said, "Good evening, Madam. Please, pardon my associate; he's shy. My name is Neil Higgins and these are my partners CatBob and Jonas Shurmann; you may know him as the Chicken-Boy of Clintonville. We request a brief audience with your feline, Blackjack."

At least that's how it happened in Neil's mind.

Jonas, however, saw his plump, gray friend waddle up to the woman's feet and begin meowing loudly.

"Awww, he's so sweet!" The woman bent down and petted his round head. "I just want to eat him up!"

Jonas nodded in agreement. "Yeah. Can we see Blackjack?" he mumbled.

"Blackjack? Oh, sure! Let me go get her." The

woman disappeared into the house.

Neil looked up at Jonas. "Was that so difficult?"

"See," Neil sniffed, "was that so difficult?"

CatBob came forward when he saw the woman return, holding the lithe black cat in her arms.

"Some of your friends have come to visit, Blackjack," she chirped. She sat the inky feline on the porch and smiled at the visitors. "Well, have fun! Just knock when you're done playing," she said as she shut the door.

"I will," Jonas answered. "Thank you."

Blackjack looked surprised to see the three detectives again.

"You?!" she gasped. "I thought the Beast had gotten you." She craned her head to look into the street. "Or are you here to tell me it's been caught? Is the curfew over? Did you find Tiger?" Blackjack's whip-like tail stood on end.

"We did find Tiger and he *is* safe," CatBob said, "but he can't return home until the Beast is caught. That's why we're here, to ask for your help."

"*My* help?" Blackjack asked. "Why would you want the help of a coward like me?" She hung her head. "I wasn't brave enough to save Tiger in the first place, remember?"

"You may have suffered a moment of weakness, or poor judgment, my dear," Neil said, "but that can't be changed now, so there's no use dwelling upon it. Now is the time to change your tomorrow."

Blackjack raised her head and swished her tail back and forth.

"That's right!" Jonas chimed in. "We need the help of someone who wants to give the neighborhood a tomorrow free of the Beast. A safe place for all cats." Jonas crouched and ran his hand gingerly down her velvety spine. "What would you be willing to do to make the neighborhood safe again, Blackjack?"

"Anything," she answered.

Neil fixed his amber eye on the inky feline. "Even if it was a dangerous mission?" he asked.

Blackjack took a deep breath and answered, "Yes."

After sunset, Clintonville was a feline ghost town, save the alley where Blackjack and CatBob stalked. The two were weaving their way through puddles when CatBob stopped to lick his side.

"Quit licking!" Blackjack scolded. "You're going to lick all the chicken juice off before the Beast has a chance to smell it."

"I can't help it," CatBob mumbled between licks, "it's too delicious! Do you want some?"

"No thanks," Blackjack thwacked her tail on the

ground in disgust. "I have my own."

"Are you sure? There's a spot on my chest that smells extra delicious, but my tongue won't quite reach it," he said as he brushed against her.

"Ewww!" Blackjack yowled. "Keep your chicken juices off of me."

CatBob laughed. He lunged and tried to hug her. "But we're wearing the same juices from the same chicken, are we not?" he asked. "I've licked all of mine off. I need a second coat!"

"Too bad!" she shot back. "You'll just have to hope the Beast likes stinky cat breath."

"Stinky?!" CatBob said scampering after her. "That was mean. I was playing and you were being mean!"

The pair frolicked around a bend in the alley where they were suddenly bombarded by a flurry of strange noises. A No Outlet sign sign loomed before them. Odd whines and rattles echoed from the shadows on all sides. The felines peered into the gloom, trying to identify the source of the sounds, but the phantom responsible seemed to dissolve into the blackness before they could see it.

"I don't like this," Blackjack whispered. "Let's go back." She turned to retreat when a growl boomed from the darkness. The gravel under her paws shook. Daring not to move a muscle, she whispered back to

CatBob, "Where is it?"

CatBob whined a warning and arched his back. His eyes were locked on a mangy snout that emerged His eyes were locked on the mangy snout that emerged from the murk like a rusty knife. Two amber eyes darted back and forth from him to Blackjack. Its jaws framed a smile of gnashing teeth. The gaunt figure crouched before CatBob, bringing its gaze level with his. The peachy feline gave no ground in the face of the brute's challenge.

"CatBob?" Blackjack whispered.

"Don't turn around," he said. "You remember the way back?"

"Yes," she said, "but you'll be with me, won't you?"

He crouched low. "When I say, just run as fast as you—"

CatBob's words were cut short by a terrific bark. Incoherent screams and the sound of pitched gravel followed.

Blackjack bolted around the bend, away from the violence.

The Beast's shifting gaze met CatBob's. The peach feline tensed every muscle in his body. He knew what was coming.

"When I say, just run as fast as you—"

He wasn't even finished speaking when the monster charged him. CatBob sprang into the air, rising level with the Beast's head.

The brute's expression of rage twisted into surprise as the airborne feline unleashed a flurry of lightning fast blows. The Beast jerked its head back so quickly that the rest of its body didn't have time to follow. Its legs slid and the animal's lanky frame collapsed into the gravel. CatBob landed on top, continuing his vicious assault until the Beast rolled to its feet, throwing him underneath its great frame.

The peach cat tried to escape, but the monster was too fast. Long white teeth pierced the flesh between his shoulder blades, lifting him off the gravel. The great jaws hoisted him up then threw him into a garage door.

He hit with a loud *bang* then sprang to his feet just in time to dodge the open jaws that bore down on him. CatBob scampered up a pile of refuse and hopped atop a trash bin. The Beast scrambled after him, but the rubbish pile refused to support its weight and sent the creature tumbling.

CatBob leapt onto a parked car and dashed across a fence to the safety of the garage roof. The Beast staggered to its feet, barking in a mad rage.

"That's it, bark all you want," CatBob taunted. "You'll never get up here. Go ahead, do your worst.

I got all night."

The Beast abandoned its attempts to snatch the sniffing the ground in search of an easier target. The brute stopped, tilted its head back, and howled at the sky.

"No, no, no!" CatBob yelled. "Come after *me*, you flea bitten mutt—"

But it was no use. The monster disappeared around the bend.

CatBob climbed down and followed as quickly as he could, but his leg and shoulder had been injured during the battle. He winced with every limp, but forced himself on. Blackjack's life was in grave danger.

Blackjack listened to the patter of her paws on the asphalt as she ran. She was already a block away when a hollow howl swept down from the garage rooftops and cast a chill over her.

She felt so weary she considered curling up where she stood and sleeping for an entire night. That is, until another sound caught her attention—the sound of thick claws scattering gravel. Blackjack looked back and saw the salivating jaws of the Beast charging toward her. She turned and bolted.

She ran into Moors Avenue where she was blinded by a bright light and barely avoided the wheels of a speeding scooter. A cacophony of screeching tires and honking noises erupted behind her as she ran pell-mell into the night. Her eyes readjusted moments later and she turned into the alley behind Nightshade Road and vanished into the darkness.

The scooter swerved, narrowly avoiding the Beast as it bolted from the mouth of the alley. The driver shouted as he struggled to bring the vehicle to an upright stop. He turned around and directed the headlight onto the animal he'd nearly struck.

"What kind of dog is that?!" the passenger shouted.

Two glowing eyes floated in the headlight beam above a grin of dagger-like teeth.

"Whoa!" The driver pounded on the horn and cranked the grip, revving the noisy engine. "Get out of here!" he shouted. "Go on—*get*!"

The Beast slunk away from the bright light and jarring noises. It broke into a run and disappeared down Moors Avenue.

"Was that a wolf?!" the passenger asked.

"Don't know," the driver shouted back. "It came from over there." He pointed toward the alley. "Looked like it was chasing that black cat."

He guided the scooter into the mouth of the alley where he could barely make out a small figure running toward them. The driver flipped up the visor of his helmet to get a better look at the approaching figure.

"CatBob?" he called.

The peach-colored feline hobbled up to the scooter, meowing frantically.

"He's hurt," the passenger said.

The driver leaned over and picked up the limping cat and examined him. Although he had obviously been roughed up, the expression on CatBobs's face wasn't one of suffering, or fear, but of a steadfast determination.

"I think he's trying to save that black cat," the driver shouted as he handed the peachy feline to his passenger.

"You're kidding me, right?!"

"Just hold on to him!" the driver commanded.

The scooter revved up and lurched into motion.

CatBob sank his claws into his handler's leather-clad shoulder and watched the road ahead.

21
THE HOME STRETCH

Blackjack couldn't catch her breath. The muscles in her haunches burned and her body felt like it was cast of lead. She slowed to a walk and looked back toward the mouth of the alley. She was alone. The anxiety that had been constricting her chest began to relax. She took in a big gulp of crisp night air.

Then a buzzing noise caught her attention. She turned to see the scooter she'd barely avoided only moments before make a sharp turn into the alley. The vehicle's headlight illuminated the entire passage, including the thing she'd failed to detect seconds before.

The lanky silhouette of the Beast was racing toward her. Fear griped her body like an icy fist. She turned and bolted down a narrow drive toward Dusenbury Street.

Just a little farther, she said to herself. *Do it for Tiger.*

Jonas scanned the empty street through his binoculars. "Nothing yet, Neil," he announced from a third-floor balcony.

Neil gave a slow blink. He sat directly across from the opening in the hedges in Orville Dusenbury's yard. If his plan worked, he would soon be face-to-face with the Beast.

He looked toward the house, where Mrs. Shurmann stood cradling a rifle in her tattooed arms. The stoic feline slowly blinked to her and then turned his attention to her husband. Mr. Shurmann and Orville Dusenbury stood before him, flanking the opening in the hedges. Each grasped the end of a thick rope that was draped over a massive tree branch and connected on the opposite end to a large net spread in the grass before the opening.

"There they are!" Jonas shouted. "Everyone get ready."

He could see Blackjack charging down a narrow drive with the Beast bearing down on her. A scooter emerged from the alley a moment later, buzzing furiously behind them. As the scooter closed in, Jonas noticed the passenger was holding something in her arms. Although the lack of light made the object difficult to identify, Jonas knew in his gut what it was.

He brought his lenses back to the small feline just as she tripped and was sent tumbling across the pavement. "Oh, no—Blackjack!" he cried.

The Beast's jaws opened wide as it bared down on the prone feline.

The driver wrenched the throttle and his fist and yelled to his passengers to hold on. The scooter lurched forward and pulled alongside the Beast. Something flew toward the massive animal and a yowl rose above the buzzing engine.

The scooter reached the end of the drive and slid sideways, zipping east toward Moors Avenue amid a chorus of car horns.

Blackjack watched a succession of images flash before her eyes: the night sky through a canopy of tree branches, a blur of asphalt, the scooter's headlight, and the Beast's open jaws. She was tumbling out of control.

Her limbs had become too tired to keep up the pace, and she'd stumbled. The slender feline tried to regain her footing, but she was rolling too fast. With each tumble the Beast's jaws got closer, the buzzing of the engine grew louder, and the headlight beam shone brighter. For a brief moment Blackjack resigned herself to her fate in the jaws of the monster, but then she noticed a change in the Beast's face—it was suddenly covered by orange fur. She heard the brute yowl as its great body slammed into her, sending her sliding into the grass, where she came to rest in a bank of leaves.

Blackjack staggered to her feet and found the Beast writhing on the pavement, flailing its legs and barking ferociously.

She crept closer and saw that the orange fur on the Beast's face was CatBob! The peach feline was hugging the brute's face and snout while his teeth inflicted bloody vengeance.

The Beast flipped over and stood up. It shook its head violently, loosening CatBob's grip and sending him crashing into the sidewalk. The detective tumbled across the pavement and rolled to a stop.

He didn't get up.

"CatBob!" Blackjack gasped.

The Beast turned to the black cat and gnashed its terrible teeth before lunging. Blackjack leaped backward and darted into Dusenbury Street. Car horns blared as she frantically zig-zagged her way around swerving and screeching tires with the Beast's jaws snapping only inches behind her.

"Here they come!" Jonas yelled.

"Three..." He began to countdown.

Orville and Mr. Shurmann gripped the rope in their fists and readied themselves.

"...Two..."

Blackjack and the Beast raced to the sidewalk, headed straight for the hedges.

"...One..."

A whirlwind of dried leaves exploded from the hedgerow as Blackjack shot from the opening, followed by her pursuer.

Neil stared straight ahead as Blackjack turned a second before colliding with him. His field of vision was then filled by the savage countenance of the Beast.

Neil peered into amber eyes that were possessed by rage. The monster's jaws opened, dripping with the anticipation of murder. Its great body bore down on the gray cat like a speeding locomotive, yet, the stoic feline refused to even flinch.

"...Now!" Jonas screamed.

Orville and Mr. Shurmann yanked the ropes with all their might. The Beast's jaws snapped shut a mere inch from Neil's face when the taut lines sent the net springing up from the grass. It closed around the creature like a grasping hand, sending it up and over Neil's head.

The brute thrashed and barked. Mrs. Shurmann aimed her rifle and fired into the writhing mass of rope and fur. The red dart found its mark in the animal's side.

Mr. Shurmann and Orville struggled to keep the brute airborne while the tranquilizer took effect, but after a few strenuous minutes, Jonas's mom gave the okay to lower the net.

Once the sedated animal had been loaded into her van and Jonas had retrieved CatBob, they all headed to the vet's office.

22
CASE CLOSED

Everyone was relieved when Mrs. Shurmann announced that CatBob was going to be okay. She explained that he was only being treated for minor wounds and some swelling. Blackjack was especially relieved by the news and begged Jonas to take her back to see him.

Jonas ushered his friends into the back room where they found CatBob sitting in an observation pen. Jonas dropped Blackjack and Neil in the corral and the pair rushed to the peachy feline, smothering him with head licks and face rubs.

"I'm so happy you're okay," Blackjack exclaimed, "You saved me—twice!"

"That's nothing. You saved all of the cats in the neighborhood," CatBob said. "Now they can roam freely without worry of the Beast, all thanks to you."

"Hey, CatBob. Who were those people on the scooter?" Jonas asked.

"That was lucky, huh?" CatBob pushed his cheeks forward into a smile. "Let's just say Orville Dusenbury and the Shurmanns aren't the only friends we cats have around here."

Jonas's mom confirmed that the Beast was, in fact, a coyote, as Orville had suspected. Although it was suffering from malnutrition, dehydration, and some nasty bites and scratches, she expected it to make a full recovery.

"That's great, but where will it go after it's recovered?" Orville asked. "I mean, it can't be allowed to roam free. The city's as dangerous for the Beast as the Beast is for the neighborhood cats. On the other hand, it wouldn't be fair to kill an animal just for trying to survive."

Mrs. Shurmann agreed. "There are coyote rescue organizations that handle situations just like this," she said. "I plan on contacting a few in the morning."

It was then that Mr. Shurmann silently directed his wife's and Orville's attention to Jonas, who was bent down with his ear next to Neil's face. They all exchanged secretive smiles.

Jonas turned to them and announced that Neil wanted to thank everyone for their participation in his plan. Thanks to their combined effort, the Beast had been apprehended and Clintonville was safe once more.

Mr. and Mrs. Shurmann laughed to one another, but stopped when they noticed Orville looking at them, perplexed.

"Well," Mr. Shurmann stammered, "we're both impressed with this plan that you and Jonas engineered, but—"

"It wasn't *my* idea," Orville said brusquely.

Mr. and Mrs. Shurmann looked over at their son, who was shaking his head.

"Neil?" Mrs. Shurmann asked.

"Neil." Jonas and Orville confirmed in unison.

The front page of *Clintonville Weekly* read, Chicken-Boy and Crime Cats Capture Coyote. The day after the edition came out, Miss Keys read the article to Jonas's class.

It said that after Jonas's mom had given the coyote a clean bill of health, arrangements were made for the animal to be handed over to a rescue organization in Indiana. When Miss Keys had finished, the class applauded, but Jonas was embarrassed by the attention.

He'd wanted to be a hero because he thought it would make people like him, but he'd learned being a hero had nothing to do with being liked. He was happy to know he could be heroic when the need arose, but he didn't do it to get his picture in the paper. Nor did he do it for the admiration of his classmates. He realized he'd even forgotten about the reward money. Jonas had assisted those who needed his help because it was the right thing to do. Having the neighborhood safe for his cat-friends once again was all the reward he wanted.

After school, Jonas was late getting to his mom's office because every cat he encountered along the way came running to the end of its walkway to greet him. And although he wasn't wearing his chicken costume that day, he knew what they were up to. Anyone could see that they were showing their gratitude to the Chicken-Boy of Clintonville for finding the missing cats and ridding the neighborhood of the Beast.

While visiting with one of the thankful felines, Jonas noticed a group of boys on the corner watching him and talking among themselves. One of the boys walked over—it was Danny Martin.

"Do they always come to see you like this?" Danny asked.

"No," Jonas said, "I think they're just really happy to be rid of the Beast. Now they can go outside again."

Danny extended his hand to the cat. It approached and sniffed his fingers.

"I'm not much of a cat person," he said. "My dad's allergic, so we we're not allowed to have one."

"Well, you're doing it right," Jonas said. "Always let them sniff your hand first, and make sure your palm faces the ground," he added. "That way, they know you're friendly."

The cat butted its head against Danny's palm. He smiled and ran his hand down the cat's back.

"See, he likes you," Jonas said.

The cat arched its back under Danny's gentle strokes and purred.

"Sorry I was a jerk before," Danny muttered. "I think it's cool you're the Chicken-Boy. You're really brave to have taken on the Beast."

"It's okay," Jonas said. "Want to play football tomorrow?"

"Sure, but I want you on *my* team this time. You and Isaac are way too good together," Danny said with a laugh.

The notoriety from the newspaper article made Neil Higgins and CatBob feline celebrities, equally. Finally, Neil had the popularity for which he'd envied CatBob. But after a few days of being showered with attention, Neil found that celebrity didn't suit him. He liked the idea of being admired, but he found all of the noise that came with the attention to be a nuisance. He was a private fellow, and decided he would rather keep it that way than be in the public eye. He and CatBob had made a difference with their friend Jonas, and that's what mattered—not the attention.

And after a week of rest, Neil's peachy partner was back to greeting everyone who walked down East Valleybluff Road. But now people wanted their picture taken with one of the famous Crime Cats, which was fine by CatBob. He welcomed the extra scritches and belly rubs that his newfound fame brought him. But the real reward was seeing Cinderella back at home with her brother, Pierre. Of course, he didn't mind the attention of a certain slender black cat in whose company he was often seen.

And when Blackjack wasn't spending her time with CatBob, she was usually found playing with her neighbors, Luna and Baba, who were mightily impressed by her heroism in helping rid the neighborhood of the Beast. But no one was more impressed, or as grateful for her bravery, as her brother, Tiger.

Jonas spent the next week after school serving as a translator for the cats that Orville brought to his mom's office. Jonas's costume enabled Mrs. Shurmann to diagnose and treat the patients more quickly and effectively than she could have imagined. When they were given a clean bill of health, the Chicken-Boy of Clintonville personally delivered them to their families.

When Jonas reunited Puck with his family, the man Jonas had seen at the vet's office was so overjoyed, he began to cry. He cradled Puck in his arms, and the marbled tabby gently placed his paw on the man's mouth to quiet him. Puck was more emotional than he would admit, and Jonas could see he was getting choked up too. The reunion was even celebrated by Puck's neighbors, Garry, Oso, Tom, Boo-Boo, and Baby, who welcomed him home with a formal invitation to dinner.

Puck's family insisted Jonas accept the reward they'd posted, but he said he'd rather it be donated to Cat Welfare in the name of the Chicken-Boy and the Crime Cats. Jonas's partners had told him how the local shelter had helped many of the cats in the neighborhood find loving homes. The family agreed.

Jonas was embarrassed to be stuck taking all the credit for the safe return of the missing cats, but Orville was very clear that he wanted his name kept out of it. He was a ghost, after all.

And on some afternoons and weekends, Jonas helped that ghost fix up his haunted house. But despite all their work, the neighborhood kids remained convinced the Dusenbury House was haunted; probably because Orville and Jonas continued to use Winslow Dusenbury's medical skeleton to wave at the kids that passed by. And to this day, the Chicken-Boy is believed to be the only kid ever to have entered the Dusenbury House and survived.

"MEETING A CAT"

In the story, it was easy for Jonas to meet new cats because his costume allowed him to speak with them. But for those who don't own a magic chicken costume, here are some tips on how to meet a new cat, and hopefully make a new friend the old fashioned way.

1. Relax. Approach the cat slowly and naturally. Cats can sense when you're tense and it makes them nervous.

2. Avoid eye contact. If a cat doesn't know you, they will be offended if you look into their eyes and will likely run away. Instead, divert your focus to their ears or nose.

3. Kneel down. Slowly kneel down and extend your hand. Make sure your palm is facing the ground. This is a signal to the cat that tells them you are friendly. You can also call to the cat by its name if you know it or by using a general name like "boy," "girl," "little guy," "kitten," or "cat."

4. Wait. Now it's up to the cat to decide if they want to meet you. If the cat stops or runs away, don't be discouraged. A cat's instinct is to be suspicious of everything and everyone, so don't take it personally. Just repeat these steps the next time you see them. Eventually, they'll figure out you have good intentions.

5. Sniff. If the cat comes to you, allow them to sniff your hand with your palm still facing the ground.

6. Slow pets. If the cat doesn't run away, you should slowly pet their back or side. Don't reach for their head. Cats instinctively interpret something or someone reaching for their head as a danger.

7. Headbutt. If the cat pushes their head against your leg, it's a signal that they consider you "safe." Congratualtions! You've made a new cat-friend.

8. Be gentle. Always be gentle with your new cat-friend.

9. Toys only. If you want to play with your cat-friend, use a toy, long piece of grass, or stick. Never play using your hands as a toy—especially rough playing like you can do with a dog—because it teaches the cat that hands are for biting.

10. Read the tags. Find out where your new cat-friend lives and who the guardians are. Should your new cat-friend become injured or get into trouble, you will know who to contact.

"MISSING CAT"

If your cat-friend goes missing, you don't need a magic chicken costume to find them. You just need to keep calm, be active, and be persistent in your search. Here are some steps to help you reunite with your feline family member.

1. Stay calm. Panicking won't help you find your cat-friend. They need you to be calm and careful in your search.

2. Don't wait. Start your search as soon as you discover your cat-friend is missing.

3. Check the house. Check every room, every closet, and every hiding place your cat-friend has established.

4. Check the yard. Cats usually stay close to their home when they get out (within a three-block radius). Bring a bag or can of your cat-friend's favorite treats along to shake while you call their name.

5. Check cars. Cats will often climb up into car engines for warmth. They don't know that an engine is a dangerous place for them. If you hear meowing coming from under the hood of a car, find the car's owner and tell them. Make sure the engine isn't started until the cat is out. If the cat cannot be coaxed out, sometimes honking the horn will scare them out, but only as a last resort.

6. Check garages. Check your garage and your neighbor's garages. Cats sometimes sneak into garages when the door is open to explore and then get trapped.

7. Check large equipment. If you have trailers, tractors, or any other large pieces of equipment, check them thoroughly. They can provide a lot of hiding places for cats.

8. Check barns. Search barns, sheds, and any other freestanding structures on your property. Be sure to ask your neighbors for permission before searching their property. Asking first will show them that you are considerate and will alert them to the fact your cat-friend is missing.

9. Place the litter box outside. If you don't initially find your cat-friend by searching, don't panic. They may have been watching you from their hiding place, but were too afraid to come to you. While you move on to the next step in your search, place their litter box on the front porch with some of your dirty clothes beside it. Be sure to check the porch just after sunrise. That's when your cat-friend will most likely come to the porch to use the litter box.

10. Web sites. Now you need to post your cat-friend's information on web sites like www.petfbi.com and any social media groups for missing pets in your area (like the *Clintonville Lost and Found* group that Jonas watches). Be sure the photo you post is well-lit. List any unique physical or behavioral traits that might help strangers recognize your cat-friend. Make sure your parents provide contact information.

11. Fliers. The next step is to create a "Missing" flier that features the cat's name, a brief description (breed, fur length, unique traits), and contact information. Post them all over your area, but be sure to go back and take them down once you have found your cat-friend.

12. Call around. Call veterinary clinics in your area and let them know your cat-friend is missing. You can also call cat shelters and pounds. Make a list of them so you can check in with them daily to see if your cat-friend has been brought in.

13. Keep searching. Go out and search the yard, garages, and all neighboring properties for your cat-friend every day. After the first day, expand your search to include a larger area. Keep the litter box and clothes on the porch, and check them every day around sunrise.

14. Stay positive but be realistic. Not all cat-friends return, no matter how much searching is done. But if you've followed these steps, take heart that you've done as much as you could for your friend.

Made in the USA
Charleston, SC
05 January 2016

BULLYING
READING LOCAL MAPS

CATS ARE VANISHING...

..all over the neighborhood, but Jonas Shurmann doesn't care. He thinks cats are spoiled brats who don't appreciate anything people do for them. Jonas has bigger problems in his life: the ridiculous-looking chicken costume he has to wear to his class Halloween party, working at the vet's office after school, and his math book getting thrown into the _____ ted house. Those are

AT LEAST THAT'S WHAT JONAS THINKS, UNTIL HE DISCOVERS HE CAN HEAR CATS TALK.

Through his newfound power, Jonas befriends two cat detectives, CatBob and Neil Higgins, and together the trio sets out on a pulse-pounding adventure that leads them straight to the door of a haunted mansion that holds the chilling truth behind the disappearances.

CRIME CATS RELIEF FUND

A portion of the profit from every new copy of *Crime Cats* sold will go to the **Crime Cats Relief Fund**: a private charity that issues grants to help with medical care expenses for Clintonville's community cats.

Join us for more fun at:
crimecatsbooks.com

$8.99 US / $9.99 CAN
Mystery / Scary
RL4   AGES 08-12

ISBN 9780615984698

90000 >

9 780615 984698